Reins of Magic

R. Dawnraven

Crossed Claymore Press

Reins of Magic by R. Dawnraven
Published by Crossed Claymore Press

Copyright © 2025 by R. Dawnraven
Map & Internal Images Copyright © 2025 by R. Dawnraven
Cover Art & Design by R. Dawnraven
Edited by Michaela Choi
Formatted in Atticus

All rights reserved.

No portion of this book may be reproduced in any form without written permission from the publisher or author, except as permitted by U.S. and Canadian copyright law.

This book is a work of fiction and as such all characters and situations are fictitious. Any semblance to actual people, places, or events is coincidental.

ISBN 978-1-7389024-4-6 (paperback)

ISBN 978-1-7389024-5-3 (ebook)

Contents

Dedication	V
Content Warnings & Pronunciation	VI
Map	VII
1. Taurin	1
2. Hills	10
3. Stranger	19
4. Liander	28
5. Ride	42
6. Language	55
7. Epiphany	63
8. Storm	76
9. Hope	86
10. Lunch	96
11. Forest	106
12. Wyn-Wyn	116

13.	Moon	130
14.	Grimmst	139
15.	Search	147
16.	Euphoria	155
17.	Breakfast	163
18.	Blaze	172
19.	Ash	183
20.	Anew	196
21.	Together	206
Acknowledgements		221
Also by		222
About the author		223

A queer, cozy story with some spice for those in need!

Content Warnings & Pronunciation

Contains explicit sexual content, animal death, and detailed descriptions of horses giving birth.

Pronunciation:

Aelim (third elven gender) – ay-lim

Belim (elven female) – bay-lim

Damis (source of an elf's magical power) – dah-miss

Grimmst – grimm-st

Liander – lee-an-der

Lyrellis – lye-rell-is

Nuu – new

Matil – mah-till

Nelim (elven male) – nay-lim

Sylandris – sy-lan-dris

Tagna – tag-na

Tahter – tah-ter

Taurin – tore-in

Orik – or-ick

Vardis – var-diss (var rhymes with far)

Vernu – vurr-new

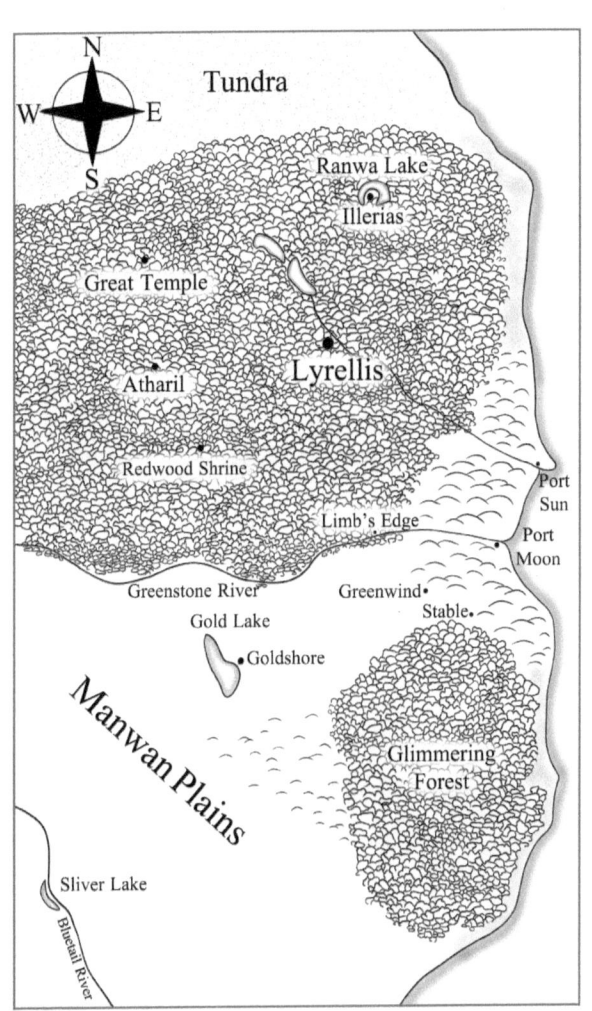

Chapter One

Taurin

It was another chilly spring morning. Birds chirped, greeting the rising sun. Taurin left his warm cottage to tend to his herd of horses and shivered. As he descended the hill to the pasture, his boots squelched in the melting snow, the last of winter's icy grip not wanting to let go. A cold breeze swept across the prairie, ruffling his long golden hair and nipping at the tips of his pointed ears.

As much as he wanted to return to the comfort of his bed with a good book, he adjusted his scarf and trudged on. The horses couldn't be ignored, especially with foaling season nearly upon them. And he needed it to be a great season, for more than his livelihood depended on it.

He quickly stopped at the chicken coop, making sure the hens were well and topping up their feed before setting them loose for the day. He'd collect their eggs once he was done with the horses.

There was one brown hen who he'd affectionately named Nellie; she had a crippled leg and had never been a good layer. The dwarves had advised against keeping her over the winter since she was an unproductive mouth to feed, but something about the sight of her uneven gait had touched his heart. Nellie clucked as she followed him all over the yard, only stopping once they reached the paddock. She never followed him inside, leading Taurin to suspect a horse had injured her leg before he'd purchased her.

The pasture was a large expanse of prairie that bordered the hills to the east, and the Glimmering Forest in the south. The fence splitting the land into several sections was made of trees and bushes whose branches had been magically woven together. It not only kept the animals in, but created a much-needed windbreak; the breeze buffeting him now was nothing compared to the howling gales that frequently swept across the Manwan Plains.

With a flick of his pale wrist, the branches before him unwound themselves, creating an opening. As he slipped through, they wove back together behind him. Dark shapes dotted the flat grassland before him. Taurin did a quick count of the mares but noticed a few were missing. Hopefully, they were grazing on the wet grasses further out. Taurin brought his fingers to his mouth and let out a loud whistle, calling on his innate magic to carry the sound.

Heads lifted.

The dots he could see started to amble towards him, tails swishing. As they got closer, he realized his most prized mare wasn't among them. Taurin frowned, his keen brown eyes watching to see if the missing horses would wander in from the furthest reaches of the field.

After a few moments, more dark shapes appeared, coming up a small slope in the land. All were accounted for. Taurin let out a breath of relief. He couldn't afford to lose any of them.

The mares surrounded him, pawing the ground with their hooves and nickering.

"Yes, yes, I know you want your treats." From within the pockets of his coat, he produced a handful of carrots. A chestnut mare snorted and tried to snatch one.

"Behave, Breeze," he chastised, patting her on the neck. He handed out the carrots, appeasing the herd. Only his quick elven reflexes prevented them from knocking him into the sloppy snow in their excitement. Yes, coming into the pasture with a handful of snacks was foolish, but the fence was too high and too tightly woven for him to give them out from the safety of the other side. Besides, he loved his herd.

Carrots consumed, the mares resumed their grazing. Taurin walked among them, checking each for any signs of injury or discomfort. Only four were pregnant; he hadn't been able to secure many breeding contracts since being given charge of the stable back in the summer. Besides, he couldn't handle that many foals on the ground at once. He alone worked the stable, and he was not the most knowledgeable in horse husbandry.

Sparrow, the mare with a reddish body and black on her legs, mane, and tail, was walking with a slight limp.

"Oh no." Taurin lifted her front hoof and picked a stone out of it. He frowned, unable to determine if it was bruised. She set her hoof down but didn't appear to be putting weight on it. "I'd better ask one of the dwarves to check it," he muttered to himself. Thankfully Sparrow wasn't pregnant. The extra weight of a foal wouldn't do her any favours.

Taurin spent extra time with his most prized mare, Lily, a beautiful dapple grey whose lineage ran back to the horses in the royal Sylandrian stable itself. He ran his hand along her swollen belly, wondering at the foal within.

"I hope your baby is as beautiful as you are," he murmured, rubbing her side.

Lily grunted in response.

When he eventually pulled his hand away, it was completely covered in grey fur. The spring shed was well underway, which meant he had his work cut out for him. Taurin didn't want them rolling on the ground to relieve the itch of their shedding coats—he feared it might harm the unborn foals.

Satisfied with the condition of the other mares, he checked on his two stallions in their own respective pastures, giving the impatient males and their calm companions their morning carrots. He had to keep the stallions separate so they wouldn't fight, but he ensured that each of them had a gelding to keep them company.

Taurin placed a hand on the fence and closed his eyes. From his *damis*—the source of an elf's magic located on the opposite side of their chest from their heart—he cast his aura outwards, following the flow of life through the plants, checking for breaks or holes. After a few moments, he returned to himself and opened his eyes. The fence was intact; nothing had tried to bust through it, nor had he detected any strange auras in the area. All he felt were the usual faint pulses coming from the Glimmering Forest to the south.

After refilling their hay and making sure the creek that ran through the pastures wasn't frozen (it shouldn't be at this time of the year) Taurin collected eggs returned to the stone cottage for his own breakfast. As much as he disliked working on an empty stomach, he knew that horses came first. A hot bowl of oats topped with berries on a chilly morning did wonders.

Taurin inhaled deeply, taking in the musty smell of horse and the sweet fragrance of growing plants. He couldn't wait for the dregs of snow to be gone. All the slop and muck from the melt was driving him nuts. A wet horse was one thing, but a muddy horse was another—it took ages to clean it off them, especially if they decided to roll around in it.

He had King, the dark stallion with tan around his eyes and muzzle, tied to the wooden hitching post outside the barn. The orange, semi-feral barn cat lazed on top of a bale of straw nearby. Taurin had just finished grooming King and was about to saddle him when he heard a rhythmic creaking accompanied by the thump of hooves. A wooden wagon approached, pulled by a stout black and white pony.

"Morning!" the driver called out. Her short stature and long, braided beard meant she was none other than a dwarf. *Belim*, female elves, did not grow beards.

"Good morning, Matil," he hollered in return, awkwardly slinging the well-used saddle over a rack.

"Whoa," she said to her pony before gently pulling on the reins. The pony stopped near the open stable door. "Here to deliver your books."

"Wow, those arrived faster than I expected! Thank you."

The dwarven woman lifted a heavy bundle off the bench beside her. "Watcha' reading about?"

"Horses," he said.

"Ah, suppose it never hurts to learn more about your livelihood."

"Especially when your knowledge of horses is limited to riding them, not caring for them," he said, accepting the bundle. Though he'd been here for nearly a full suncycle, he felt like he had hardly scratched the surface. Every day brought new challenges.

"That'd be true," she said with a nod.

"Speaking of, one of my mares had a rock in her hoof. I was able to remove it, but she won't put any weight on that leg. Would you mind checking it out?"

Matil was already out of her wagon, hitching her pony to a ring mounted on the barn's peeling wall. "Let's go."

"Thank you." He quickly set the books down on a bucket just inside the barn door and led her out to the pasture.

Passing through the fence, he pointed out Sparrow, who thankfully hadn't strayed far. Was it because of her injury? "She's the bay mare. See how she won't put weight on that front hoof?"

"Hmm, let's take a look." Matil strode up to the grazing mare, going slow. Most of the mares had spread out over the pasture, giving her room to work. "Hey there, girl. I hear you've got a sore foot." She held out her hand, letting Sparrow sniff it for a moment. The mare eventually grunted and resumed grazing.

"That's a good girl." Matil patted her on the neck and took a step forward so that she was beside her shoulder, facing the mare's rump. She kept petting and patting her, talking to her soothingly as she reached for the affected leg. Sparrow didn't react. She ran her hand down the leg, bending as she got low, and pinched the back of it near the base right above where it curved in above Sparrow's hoof.

Sparrow didn't lift her foot at the tactile command.

"Stubborn, eh?"

"They sometimes do that," said Taurin.

"Yeah, that's horses for you. Alright." She leaned her body against Sparrow's leg, forcing the mare to shift her weight, and squeezed again.

Sparrow flicked an ear and raised her foot which Matil held in one calloused hand.

Matil stopped leaning.

"How does it look?" asked Taurin, worrying a thread on his sleeve.

"Good news is, I don't see any bruising," she said. "I'd keep an eye on her for now and see how she is. If it gets worse, bring her inside and reach out to old Grimmst." She gently lowered Sparrow's hoof and straightened up.

"I will. Thank you for looking at it."

"No problem."

They headed back to the barn and Matil's cart.

"Do you want a drink or something to eat on the road?" asked Taurin, petting King, whom he could now return to the field.

"Naw, I'm good. I've only a few more things to drop off. You're the furthest one out."

"I'm sorry," he said with a small smile.

"Bah. It's nothing," she said as she untied her pony and hopped back up into the driver's seat. She looked around the yard. "You sure you're doing alright by yourself?"

"I'm managing."

King snorted.

They both looked at him.

"Humph. Well, if you ever get lonely, feel free to stop by! Me and Tagna will fix you up something tasty!" Matil signalled to her pony and started back towards the road—if the ruts in the soggy ground could be called that.

"I will. And thank you again!" He waved then turned his attention back to the stallion.

As Taurin led him back to the pasture, he couldn't help but worry about all the things he didn't know about horse husbandry. And while the dwarves were a huge help, Matil was right. He was rather isolated out here.

It's as if they want me to fail.

Chapter Two

Hills

Dark waves rolled across a cold, sandy beach as a figure dragged its water-logged self out of the frigid sea and flopped onto the sand. He took a few strained breaths, chest burning from his unwanted dip, triggering a bout of harsh coughing that expelled salty water from his lungs. He took a few more, his breathing slowly returning as he breathed what seemed to be his first breaths of pure air in days. Or maybe it had only been half a day. He had no idea how long he'd been tossed about the waves like a battered piece of driftwood.

He rose on unsteady legs, wet clothing clinging to him, and checked to see if anything was broken. To his relief, every bone was in place—but he still felt like he'd been run over by a cart full of rocks. Calling on his magic, he dried his sopping, heavy clothes with a warm burst of air, displeased by how much energy it took in this state. He quickly searched for any remnants of his boat, or any survivors. The beach was completely barren. He found no scrap of cloth, smashed bottles, or any bits of wood. All he had were the clothes on his back, his sword—which he needed to clean as soon as possible if he didn't want the salty water to ruin it—and the small pouch tied to the sash around his waist. The magic in the sword had saved his life, helping him keep his head above water while others around him had sunk to a watery grave.

Pushing aside the intense feeling of loss that would surely overwhelm him if he gave in to it, he flipped his long, onyx hair over his shoulder and set about scaling the cliffs that cut the beach off from the rest of the world. He would mourn his companions later, once he was away from the rising tide that would soon completely cover the sand.

Climbing was no easy task. Though his clothes were dry, his body was still frozen from the cold water and blowing wind. And he didn't want to use magic again unless he absolutely had to.

Slowly but surely, he made his way up the cliff, pausing at every ledge he could squish onto to rub feeling back into his stiff hands. Slipping and falling from these heights would be disastrous.

Rolling hills met his dark eyes as he hauled himself up over the edge. The smell of musty wet earth filled his nose, noticeably different from the salty scent of the sea that had become so familiar. He'd been hoping for a town, or even a farm, someplace warm he could beg a room for the night, but he couldn't see anything of the sort. Reaching out with his magical aura, he tried to detect others in his mind's eye. Nothing. He frowned. Either there was no one around, or he'd ended up in a place with very few magic-users.

Hopefully, it was the latter.

Turning around and looking up down the coast, he couldn't see any ports. Well, he supposed hills were better than nothing. They would at least provide some shelter from the biting spring wind.

He would have pressed on if not for the fact he'd nearly just drowned, and his body felt as if it were made of lead. He needed to rest and recuperate. Instead, he used the last of his magic to dig into the side of one of the slush-covered hills, making a small, uncomfortable shelter. Sitting done with his back pressed against the dirt wall, he immediately passed out, completely drained.

Suddenly, he awoke, damp and trembling with cold. The dark shelter was freezing; he couldn't feel his extremities. Cursing himself for not starting a fire, he quickly conjured one up, letting the light and heat warm him. By the gods, how he longed for a hot meal and a cup of tea! Anything to shake off the chill that had long settled into his bones. He glanced at the sword propped up beside him. It would be days before its magic replenished itself.

It didn't help that he felt just as tired as before. Perhaps that was a small blessing; had he slept any longer, he could have been in serious trouble. Once the feeling returned to the pointed tips of his ears, he allowed himself to fall back to sleep.

The wind had died down when he eventually emerged from his hole, and the sun was rising over the sea, endless waves gleaming and sparkling in its light. He squinted at the brightness, head throbbing. All of him hurt, which he supposed wasn't surprising given he'd been tossed around like a stick for who knows how long. He had to find a proper place to sleep; he wouldn't tolerate another night like that, nor did he think his bruised and battered body would be able to handle it.

I need a bed.

He set off into the hills, moving inland. Hunger gnawed at his belly. Hmm, when had he last eaten? At least a day ago. Maybe more. Sometime before the storm that had caused the boat to capsize. He kept an eye out for animals as he trudged through the hills. It was still too early in the season for there to be anything to forage, assuming he'd recognize any of the plants. After all, he had no idea where he was.

Not wanting to waste energy scaling each hill, he travelled close to their bases, the slopes slippery with the last traces of snow. Though, he did periodically climb one in hopes that he would see smoke or, better yet, a village. But all he ever saw were more rolling hills. That didn't bode well. Hopefully, he hadn't landed on some uninhabited island. Given what he could recall of the map that had been lost to the waves, that was very possible.

Unfortunately, he didn't have much luck finding anything to eat. Aside from birds, who flew too high up for him to catch, especially in his exhausted state, he saw neither hide nor hair of any creature. Strange. Were they still hibernating? That was a long nap if that were the case. He sighed and plodded on.

The midday sun soon passed, slowly sinking in the sky.

Damn it, I need to find shelter. He had no desire to spend another night like the last, but as the afternoon wore on, he still saw no sign of civilization. Was this land truly uninhabited by anyone save for the birds?

As the sun started to disappear below the hills, taking with it its warmth, fortune finally smiled upon him. Something glinted around one of the hills. A musky, muddy scent hit him as he hurried towards it.

A creek lazily wound itself between the slopes.

Water wasn't hard to come by; he'd been melting the slushy snow. It didn't taste great, but it was more than enough to stop his throat from becoming parched. He didn't need the creek for water. He needed it for fish—for food.

But as he approached, his heart sank. Though the creek was wide, it was shallow with a muddy bottom. With his elven eyes and aura, he found nothing aside from some minnows who were more bone than anything. A handful would hardly be a snack, never mind a meal.

I have to try. He fished some out with his magic, toasted them with a burst of flame, and popped them in his mouth. His face scrunched up as he chewed. Yup, all bones.

Picking the tiny bones from his teeth, he carried on. A muddy creek that housed such little life wouldn't lead him to a warm bed.

His stomach rumbled, but he did his best to ignore it. Yet it became harder to ignore his body's complaints as the chill of night set in, the sun slipping below the hills. Unfortunately, it looked like he would be sleeping in a hole again. His lip twitched with displeasure.

While he wasn't unfamiliar with uncomfortable nights, he wasn't used to being alone. He'd always travelled in a group of warriors. Travelling by oneself was unwise, especially in foreign lands. Who knew what could creep up on him at night—or during the day. And being alone with his thoughts was doing little for his mood. Despite his efforts to keep them pushed away, they kept creeping back to his fellow warriors who had perished on the boat. He sighed. He'd take being stuck with one of the grouchy captains back home over being alone.

The clashing of steel echoed through his mind. Well, maybe not the captains.

Still, there was nothing to distract him from the sudden sense of loss that gripped him. Things weren't supposed to have turned out like this.

As the darkness of night rolled over the land, he picked a hill and magically dug another hole. He swayed at the sudden loss of energy and all but tumbled inside before conjuring a small fire and curling up beside it. Despite his exhaustion, he hardly slept. His battered body ached all over, and hunger clawed at his stomach. This could not go on, he refused to succumb after surviving the wrath of the sea. Tomorrow, if he didn't find any signs of people, he had to find something to eat. Even if it meant more crunchy minnows.

The next day was only marginally more fruitful than the last. He managed to catch some sort of small, furry rodent, devouring it hungrily—though hardly more than a snack—after charring it with flame. Sadly, upon digging into its burrow, he found that it had been alone. His stomach rumbled in protest.

He kept an aural lookout as he walked around hill after hill. It seemed like they would never end. Was he walking in circles? Possibly, it was hard to tell out here. The stars at night seemed to be in the same positions as at home, but they didn't do him any good since he was mostly travelling by daylight when it was warmer.

But today, the sun didn't want to show its face. Heavy clouds filled the sky, threatening rain. By the gods, he couldn't afford to deal with rain. He'd have to spend the entire day in another hole, and that was the last thing he wanted. He could hardly stand the thought of doing it again tonight if he didn't find an actual building before nightfall.

Fortunately, the rain held off until dusk, but he still had to burrow into a hill like the rodent he'd eaten for lunch. He got no sleep that night either, and the meager fire couldn't fight off the damp chill sinking into his bones, or dissipate the hunger that clawed at his very being.

The rain eventually stopped. Shivering, his sluggish mind decided to continue walking. If he were going to freeze to death in these accursed hills, he'd rather it be while he was standing, not curled up like a rabbit. He had some pride, after all.

Clouds still blanketed the sky, obscuring the stars. He could just make out the faint glow of the twin moons. But it gave him an idea.

On numb feet, he climbed to the top of a hill, praying with all his being that the darkness would lead to his salvation.

He slowly turned about, searching for any pinpricks of light, any sign of a fire. Of warmth.

Nothing. Absolutely nothing.

How cruel was fate for allowing him to survive the sea only for him to perish in a strange land? His aching legs gave way, and he fell, the wet grass soaking his knees. This couldn't be the end, could it? He was a warrior; he couldn't die like this. It was so undignified. He'd always believed he would fall in battle.

Was this punishment for what he'd done? No, leaving had been the right choice. For his own sanity.

Something flickered in his peripheral. His head snapped up, his dark eyes peering through the darkness.

Is that...?

Rising on numbed legs, he headed towards the flickering light, hoping it wasn't his muddled mind playing tricks on him.

Not wanting to lose his way, he climbed hill after hill. Ever so slowly, the light grew brighter, but walking became harder and harder as the cold stole the last of his strength. His body was heavy, tired. Everything he could still feel ached, and the parts he couldn't feel, well, he hoped they were still attached.

The land flattened out. A cottage came into view, built on top of one of the blasted hills. Light flickered in a window, drawing him like a moth. His heart leapt. A few more steps, and he would be there. But a tangle of trees and bushes rose before him, their branches so tightly woven he doubted even a rodent would be able to slip through.

Gathering the last dregs of magic he could pull from the depths of his being, he pushed his way through.

Chapter Three

Stranger

Taurin rose at dawn as he did every day. Yawning, he pulled on his coat and trudged out into the yard, wishing he was curled up in bed with a hot cup of his favourite tea and a good book instead. Well, he could do that after the horses were tended to. Freezing his ass off outside would only make tea that much more enjoyable.

After loosing the hens—they were very vocal this morning, especially Nellie—he made his way down the pasture, noting that the recent rain had washed the remaining snow away, leaving behind a mess of mud. Ugh, great. He didn't know what was worse, the clean but slippery slush that soaked everything, or messy, messy, mud. He was really growing to dislike spring on the edge of the prairie; it had been much more pleasant in Lyrellis, where all the homes and buildings were high up in the immense trees, connected by walkways woven from their branches. There was none of this muck up there, and the forest helped to block the worst of the wind.

But all his grumbling disappeared as he neared the pasture. Something was wrong. The mares were gathered off to one side, nosing at a dark shape on the ground.

Taurin's mouth went dry. He flicked his hand, creating an opening in the branches, and sprinted across the field. Something had tampered with the fence, and he felt a strange aura about. He gathered up his power, ready to attack should it be some fell beast that had come to prey on his herd.

"Get away from there!" he shouted as he ran. The mares snorted at the noise. A few nervously backed away, but the thing thankfully didn't move. Had they killed it?

The dark mass took on a more definite shape as he got closer. He saw the blade of an ear, the point of a nose. The thing in the pasture wasn't a beast, but an elf. Taurin slowed, keeping his guard up.

Frowning, he cautiously approached the stranger. "Hey, you there!" he said awkwardly, trying to sound braver than he felt.

The stranger didn't stir, not even when Sparrow and Lily nosed them with their velvety muzzles.

His brown eyes flicked over them, but he couldn't see any obvious signs of injury under their strange clothes, nor any blood. Hesitantly, he reached out with his aura, touching theirs. It was incredibly weak, hardly a flutter.

Oh no.

He hooked an arm under them, wrapping one of theirs around his shoulders, and began to haul the freezing cold stranger back to the cottage. They were heavy, but Taurin persisted, he wasn't about to let them expire in his pasture. Nellie ambled behind them, clucking her opinion. She followed them all the way up the hill and, surprisingly, into the cottage.

A million questions buzzed in Taurin's mind. Who was this stranger? Where had they come from? Why was their hair black? He'd never seen anything like it before: all the elves in Sylandris had pale hair. But he pushed those thoughts aside once he laid them on the stuffed leather couch in front of the fireplace.

He snapped his fingers at the smouldering wood. Flames sprang to life, hot and bright. Taurin removed the sword from the stranger's waist. The shape of the hilt vaguely resembled a *vernu*, the giant feathered serpents that lived deep in the forest, and the straight scabbard had a pattern of dragon-like scales all over it. A large red tassel hung from the pommel. A strange aura thrummed from the weapon. What sort of enchantments had they placed on it?

With some effort, Nellie hopped up onto the wooden rocking chair, her dark eyes watching Taurin as he set about pulling off the stranger's wet travelling clothes. The garments under their cloak were strange: layers of indigo fabric that crossed over in the front, tied at the waist with a wide, embroidered sash; leggings of a similar loose material; leather bracers and greaves lined with fur.

He put a rough blanket over the stranger and went into the kitchen to put on some water for tea. He couldn't help but steal glances at them every now and then. Their features were so different from anything he'd seen in Lyrellis. Briefly, he wondered if they were indeed an elf but quickly shook away that foolish thought. Of course they were. They just had darker hair and a facial structure he simply wasn't used to.

With so many stolen glances distracting him, Taurin nearly dropped the kettle as he set it on the stove. A hot flush filled his cheeks; he was glad they hadn't seen.

While Taurin waited for the water to boil, he returned to the stranger. He reached out to touch their hand, wanting to see if they'd warmed up, but hesitated. Instead, his curiosity got the better of him, and he brushed their tangled raven hair away from their face. His heart fluttered at the sight of their chiselled cheekbones and angular jaw. By the Ancestors, they were gorgeous! He kept his hand pressed against their cheek for a heartbeat longer: it was still cold. Well, at least they didn't have a fever. He frowned and dropped his hand. What else could he do?

"I should call upon the dwarves..." Taurin wasn't the greatest at magic, so he'd have to contact them the mundane way—in person. But that meant saddling up and riding into town, which was at least an hour's hard ride away, and he didn't want to leave the stranger alone. What if they woke up? What if their condition worsened? Taurin couldn't risk it. If they took a turn for the worse, he would act, but for now, he would watch over them.

He wondered if he should remove more of their clothing, worried that it was wet too, but the thought of doing so made his face hot.

Get a hold of yourself!

Mentally chastising himself, Taurin rolled back the blanket he'd placed over the stranger and felt their sleeve. Damp.

His brow furrowed in concern. He had no choice.

Ever so carefully, he peeled off the stranger's layers. He did his best not to look at their broad bare chest, but the sharp curves and lines of hardened muscles drew his eye. Pulling his attention away, Taurin rolled up one of the legs of their pants to see if they had a layer on underneath before removing them as well. Soon, they were in nothing but their white underclothes.

A sharp whistling split the air.

Taurin jumped. Quickly but carefully, he covered the stranger with the blanket and hurried to the stove to make tea. As he did, he glanced out the window facing the pasture. Ugh. He still needed to check the fence and tend to the horses.

Taurin poured the water into a pink floral pot and covered it to steep before quickly pulling on his coat and hurrying outside.

When he returned to the house a bit later, the stranger hadn't moved, but Nellie had made herself at home on their chest. Taurin's first instinct was to shoo her away, but decided against it. She was helping to keep them warm.

He reached out to touch the stranger's hand and was met with a sharp pain.

"Hey!" He looked at Nellie, who was watching him like a hawk, ready to peck him again. "I'm just trying to help!"

After convincing her that he meant no harm, he checked the stranger's hand, noting that it felt marginally warmer, then set about making some breakfast. He prepared enough for them both, just in case the stranger woke up. Sitting in the wooden rocking chair near the fire with his meal, Taurin tried to focus on his food and not his guest. His nearly naked guest.

His face burned.

Taurin kept a close eye on them as he set about doing his household chores. Unfortunately, he soon needed to head back outside. With the rain they'd had, he wanted to bring the three pregnant mares and Sparrow into the stable and give them a good brushing. They weren't as sensitive to the cold and damp as he was, but he didn't want to risk their foals. Or Sparrow's hoof. Too much was riding on the births, especially Lily's. Her foal was the one he was looking forward to most of all.

Casting a worried glance at the elf and the protective hen on the couch, he donned his coat again and went outside.

Grooming the mares took much longer than he had anticipated. The mud was still wet, so he couldn't simply brush it off. Conjuring a spray of warm water, he carefully washed each one, taking time to clean Sparrow's bruised hoof. Her limp wasn't improving as much as he'd like. He'd have to send for Grimmst.

He thoroughly dried each of the mares with towels and bursts of air. Would they be muddy again within minutes of returning to the pasture? Probably. But there was nothing he could do about it. The field was likely going to be a mess for at least half a moon unless they got some unusually warm, sunny weather.

For his own peace of mind, he decided to let the four mares sleep in the warm barn tonight.

"You behave, alright?" he told them as he shut the door.

Taurin didn't sleep well that night, worried about his guest. The elf hadn't stirred once all day, and showed no signs of waking as the sun set. But the fire had warmed them, and Taurin couldn't detect a fever brewing. Their aura, though foreign, seemed stable and was growing stronger. Nellie was still perched upon their chest.

He forced himself to climb the narrow stairs up to bed, instead of trying to sleep in the rocking chair. Yet he couldn't help but lay awake. What if they took a turn during the night? What if they woke up and tried to do...something? *Nellie would make a fuss if they woke.* The two moons were high in the sky before sleep claimed him.

As he descended the stairs the next morning, rubbing sleep from his eyes, he heard an alarmed squawk. Suddenly wide awake, he hurried into the sitting room.

The stranger was sitting up on the couch, looking at the floor in confusion. Nellie clucked indignantly on the ground between the couch and the small table.

"Good morning," Taurin said, hopefully not sounding as tense as he felt. So preoccupied with their condition, he hadn't thought about what he would do once the stranger woke up.

"Morning," they said, voice hoarse like it hadn't been used in a while.

Their eyes met. Taurin's stomach fluttered. Their—his—eyes were so dark that it felt like he was being drawn into them.

"How are you feeling? I found you unconscious in my pasture." Taurin stepped closer and scooped up Nellie. He gently patted her back, calming her down. Now that the newcomer was awake, suspicion crept into his mind. Why had the stranger been out there? Was he after the horses?

"Ah, I'm sorry about that." His words had a lilt to them Taurin had never heard before. The stranger looked down at his hands. "I was lost in the hills and saw the light from this cottage."

Oh? "So you're not here to steal my horses?" Taurin gently set Nellie on the rocking chair and set about relighting the fire, careful not to fully turn his back on his guest. Thankfully, the tasselled sword was leaning against the wall, out of reach.

"No, not at all. The last thing I remember is..." He thought for a moment. "Following the light and breaking through some sort of ward."

The paddock fence.

The thought seemed to occur to the stranger. "Ah—I hope none of your horses escaped?"

With a snap of his fingers, a flame jumped to life on the wood Taurin had just put in. "They're all accounted for. They were very curious about the thing lying on the ground. Tea?"

"Tea sounds good." The stranger's stomach rumbled loudly.

"Breakfast, too, I suppose. My name is Taurin."

"Liander, but you may call me Li. Any food you can spare would be much appreciated."

Chapter Four

Liander

As his saviour disappeared into the small kitchen, Liander lay back down on the worn leather couch and closed his eyes. The scent of cooking eggs soon drifted out from it, mixing with the smoky smell of the fire. His stomach grumbled; he couldn't wait for a proper meal.

A weight landed on his middle and he cracked open an eye to see the brown hen making herself comfortable. He made no effort to shoo her away as his mind slowly pieced together fragments from his time at sea. He and a handful of others had boarded the ship and sailed for days. He couldn't recall any other boats pursuing them, friend or foe. They'd been sailing east…? Yes, east. Then, the storm had struck up out of nowhere. Howling winds and the crashing of waves had filled his ears. He remembered salt stinging his eyes and tongue—the sea. Magical auras had whirled around him, dizzying flashes of colour in his mind's eye.

Li frowned. At the time, he'd thought he'd felt auras of elves he'd left back on the mainland, but had chalked it up to the overwhelming forces of the elements messing with all his senses. But now...maybe those auras had been present. Had they conjured up the storm? With enough sorcerers, it was possible. Something unpleasant settled in his stomach. Perhaps it was a good thing he hadn't eaten yet.

Needing a distraction, he sat up, careful not to disturb the brown hen, and looked around the room, trying to build an image of his host. The cottage he found himself in was small. The main floor consisted of the kitchen, the sitting room he was currently in, and a door that led to the washroom. Stairs led up to the second floor where Taurin slept. The main floor was rather barren. Aside from the simple set of old furniture and a shelf full of books, there wasn't much in the way of decor. It gave the impression that Taurin hadn't been here long, or, perhaps he planned on leaving soon. Either way, everything was neat and tidy. The only thing that stood out was the small leather-bound book that lay closed on the rocking chair. A small bottle of ink and a quill on the wooden table between them.

He lay back on the couch, frowning as his body and the chicken protested the movement. He felt like he'd been run over by a horse—which was very possible given where he'd been found. But the chill was gone from his body, and there was a roof over his head. Soon, his host would return with something warm to fill his belly. Li was lucky. So, so lucky. Who knows how long he could have wandered lost in the hills? Li let out a small sigh and closed his eyes, gently petting the hen's soft feathers.

Now that his survival was no longer on the line, grief threatened to rise up. His heart panged, and tears welled in the corners of his eyes as he thought about those who'd perished when the boat had capsized. They had all been warriors like him. Some he'd known for decades, having trained together. It was like losing a family member. He bit his lip to keep quiet, not wanting to disturb Taurin with his grief. Silently, he let the tears fall. He wished he had their bodies, but none had washed up on the beach with him. Once his strength had returned, he would find a way to properly honour their passing.

"Do you want honey in your tea?" Taurin called from the kitchen.

Li blinked away the last of his tears. "Yes, thank you." He sat back up, smoothing his features. He could see his host through the doorway as Taurin bustled about the kitchen, plating the eggs and pouring mugs of tea.

Though he tried not to, it was hard not to stare at the golden elf. Li had never seen hair like that before, bright as sunlight. Did all the elves in this land look like him? Everyone back home had dark hair. Just where was he? Perhaps Taurin had a map.

"Do you need any help?" Li asked, lifting the hen—who clucked unhappily—and pushing the blanket off him. He blinked, realizing he was in his underclothes. Well, that wasn't surprising. Was Taurin the one who had undressed him, or was someone else around? He had so many questions...his stomach rumbled loudly, the earlier queasiness gone. They could wait until after he'd eaten.

"I'm alright," said Taurin, coming over with a steaming mug of tea. "Careful, it's hot."

Li set the hen on the floor and gratefully accepted it, inhaling its scent. The tea had a rich, earthy smell, different from what he was used to but not unpleasant.

Taurin returned to the kitchen, then came out with a plate of seasoned eggs and a hunk of bread. "I'm sorry, it's not much," he said, not meeting Li's eyes.

"It's more than I've had the past few days."

"We can talk about that once I've tended to the horses." He pulled on a long coat. "I'll be back in a bit. Feel free to help yourself to what's left on the stove."

"Thank you," Li said as Taurin walked out the door.

Slowly, Li ate his meal, resisting the urge to scarf it all down; it would only upset his stomach if he did. He fed little bits to the hen who had settled in his lap.

Once his plate was clear of every speck of egg and crumb of bread, Li moved the bird off him, dropped his legs over the edge of the couch and rose to his feet. Everything ached, but the room didn't spin as he anticipated. He wandered into the kitchen, closely followed by his feathered guardian, and looked for more food. Another serving of eggs was still in the iron pan, but he left it. Taurin had said he could help himself but Li didn't want to deprive him of his breakfast, especially not after tending to horses. He would know—he'd looked after horses himself.

Li peered out the kitchen's small window, giving him a decent view of the wet field below. Taurin released a few horses into the herd, the morning sunlight glinting off his golden hair. His heart skipped a beat. Was it as soft as it looked?

Restless, he sought out his clothes, which Taurin had thoughtfully hung to dry by the fire, though the outer layers were still muddy. Early morning sunlight greeted him as he pulled them on and opened the door.

The stone cottage was built atop a small hill with a walkway of pebbles leading down to the yard. There was a small barn, a storage shed, and a chicken coop. All looked in need of repair, but the barn was the worst. He could see holes in the roof.

"You coming?" he asked over his shoulder to the hen. She waddled towards him on uneven legs.

As he and the bird descended the hill, Li was hit with the smell of wet grass and the musk of horses. Immediately, he was reminded of riding with the other warriors back home. Of the missions they had undertaken to protect their realm. A wave of sadness pierced his heart, tears pricking at the corners of his eyes. Those rides would never happen again. He sighed, shoulders drooping. Things shouldn't have ended up like this. Yet he didn't regret boarding the boat. He'd accepted the risks when he'd stepped onto the dock.

"Li! Are you sure you should be out?" Taurin called, pulling him from his spiralling thoughts.

He blinked away his tears and straightened up, not wanting his host to see him in such a state. "I wanted to get some air and stretch my legs," he said, approaching the tightly woven fence.

"I figured I would come meet your herd." He glanced around to see if any stable hands were about, but only saw Taurin. He didn't sense any other auras.

"Give me a moment. I'll let you in." Taurin pushed through the mares and pressed a hand to the fence. The branches around it quivered and pulled away, creating an opening large enough for Li.

He felt traces of Taurin's aura as he passed through. It was very much like the aura of the elves back home. Not that he had doubted that Taurin was an elf. But with his light features, he wondered if perhaps their magic was different.

The hole in the fence remained, Taurin leaving him a quick way out if needed. Li wasn't worried. He'd spent most of his life with horses, and the mares seemed to sense it. They approached with their ears pricked forward, bopping him with their muzzles. Petting the soft velvet of their noses, he let them take in his scent. He probably didn't smell great after being thrown about the sea and wandering the hills, but the animals wouldn't care.

"I think they recognize me as the thing you found in the field." A bay mare bobbed her head as he scratched the side of her neck. "I probably smell a bit like them after lying in the mud the other night."

"I suppose," said Taurin. "I'm just glad they didn't trample you to death. Mares can be temperamental."

"Yes, they can."

"You've been around horses before?"

"Spent most of my life with them," Li said. "Riding is one of the most basic skills for a warrior."

Taurin blinked.

Hmm, perhaps he should have kept that to himself. No, Taurin likely already suspected he could fight. He'd been carrying an enchanted sword, after all.

"Do you work here alone?" Li asked. "I haven't seen anyone else."

Taurin started handing out carrots to the mares, which caused them all to swarm him. Li nimbly moved aside so he didn't get knocked over.

"Yes, it's just me. I'm working to build this place into a reputable breeding stable for Lyrellis."

Lyrellis. That wasn't a name he recognized. "Is that a person, or...?"

Taurin doled out the rest of the carrots. "Lyrellis is the royal city. Once I've checked on the stallions, we can go back inside and talk over something warm."

Something warm was a good idea. The damp morning air was starting to creep into his bones. How had he survived in the hills?

"So, what were you doing in the pasture?" Taurin asked, sitting in the rocking chair with another mug of dark, fragrant tea.

Li sat on the couch, letting his mug warm his hands. Nellie was tucked up beside him, to both of their surprise. "It's a bit of a story, but I was travelling across the sea with some of my fellow warriors, and a storm hit us." He left out some details, like why he'd left home and the fact that the storm had been magically conjured. Taurin may have saved him, but that didn't mean Li could trust him yet. "The boat capsized, and I washed up on a beach—alone and without any supplies. I scaled the cliffs and wandered through the hills for days. Eventually, I saw the light of your home and passed out in the field."

"I'm sorry to hear that," said Taurin, looking genuinely saddened.

Li felt a pang of guilt. Strange, why was he feeling guilty? Was it because he was the only survivor or because he wasn't being honest with his host? Either way, it was rather unlike him. Perhaps it was just the stress and exhaustion of the past few days making him emotionally unstable. As a warrior, he'd learned to temper his emotions, to conceal them, especially from enemies who could exploit them. He took a sip of his tea, the drink warming him.

"Where will you be going?" Taurin asked.

"I'm not sure," Li answered, "These lands are new to me."

"I see. Well, you've landed in Sylandris. I have a map somewhere you can look at. If that will help."

Sylandris. It was west across the sea. As far as Li knew, they didn't do any trade with Sylandris, but that wasn't his area of expertise. "I would greatly appreciate that."

His host set down his tea and went upstairs. Several thumps came from the ceiling above Li's head before Taurin returned.

"Here." He unfurled a battered map on the small wooden table between them.

Li's mouth tightened. He didn't recognize the landmass presented, and the writing was a little strange. It resembled his native script, but some of the labels he couldn't decipher.

"This is Lyrellis," said Taurin, pointing to a large dot in the forested part. "And we're here." He moved his hand southeast, closer to the sea. "We're just north of the Glimmering Forest, and west of the hills. Sometimes if you concentrate hard under one of the full moons, you can feel traces of the forest's aura."

"Then I must have washed up somewhere along here." Li went to tap the coastline east of the hills and brushed his hand against Taurin's. He quickly pulled back, heat flashing through him.

Taurin didn't seem to notice. He removed his hand from the map, skin smoother than Li would expect from someone who raised horses. How long had he been out here? His own hands were callused from wielding his sword.

"That makes the most sense, given how long it took you to get here from the beach. Where did you sail from?"

"I came from the east, possibly the southeast, across the ocean." The map ended at the eastern sea, showing nothing of the lands beyond. He sipped his tea. "My homeland is known as the Land of Cascading Clouds."

Taurin raised a brow. "That's quite the name."

"It's more commonly referred to as the Cloud Empire."

"That doesn't sound familiar," said Taurin apologetically, "but I was never one for proper study. I prefer stories over academic texts."

"And I prefer the sword to any sort of reading." Their eyes met. Li's heart skipped a beat. Damn, his host was gorgeous. He dropped his gaze back to the wrinkled map. "Is this the closest port city?" He pointed to the only dot along the coast, unable to read the name.

"Yes, Port Moon is the closest. It belongs to the dwarves. The one further up the coast belongs to us."

Li blinked. "Dwarves?"

"You know, short folk with round ears and facial hair."

"I know what dwarves are," Li said flatly. "But I've never seen one in person before. There aren't many back home, only in scrolls and stories." His curiosity was piqued.

"They live all over the plains," Taurin explained. "They stop by occasionally to deliver supplies since I'm a tad isolated out here."

Li perked up at that. Taurin lived alone? "I'd like to meet them."

"Old Grimmst should be by any day now to check Sparrow's foot. She had a rock in it, and her limp hasn't completely gone away yet. If you're still here when he comes, I'll introduce you."

If you're still here. Li had no desire to return to his homeland. There was nothing there for him anymore. "If you don't mind," Li started slowly, a little unsure of his own idea, "I'd like to stick around a bit longer. I can help you out with the horses." He had nowhere else to go. Once he was more familiar with the land and its people, he would move on.

His saviour gave him a questioning look, likely wondering why he wasn't eager to leave, but didn't pursue it. "I certainly could use the extra hands, though I have no coin to pay you."

"Warm food and a roof over my head will be more than enough," said Li. "And more of this tea."

Taurin smiled, dazzling him. "Alright, it's a deal."

The next morning, Li found himself on the roof of the barn, patching holes with lumber Taurin had bartered from the dwarves. His magic hadn't fully recharged, but he didn't mind doing it all by hand. It felt good to use his muscles, even if they still ached.

"I offered the dwarves one of the four foals in exchange for materials," said his host over breakfast. "They're looking forward to adding new blood to their lines."

Taurin had tried to convince him that he didn't need help with the barn, that he should rest a bit longer, but that didn't sit well with Liander. He was feeling revitalized after a few good meals and some solid rest. Sitting around the cottage wouldn't do either of them any good—not when Li had room and board to earn.

Taurin was inside, patching holes and refinishing the six wooden stalls and tiny tack room that was no more than a glorified closet. "It was very drafty all winter," he explained. "I'd wanted to fix it sooner but didn't have enough resources..." Meaning he hadn't had anyone around to help. Despite the barn's poor condition, the horses had fared well over the winter; their thick coats had protected them from the worst of the cold.

Li worked until the spring sun was high in the sky, only stopping when Taurin called him for a break.

"Here, have something to eat." Taurin handed him a generous slice of bread from the loaf he'd baked the day before and a hunk of cheese.

They sat on a small bench in the barn. Taurin's shoulder accidentally brushed Li's as he turned, and the touch sent sparks of heat through him, making his pulse race. There was nothing strange about what they were doing. He'd shared many meals with other warriors in even more cramped conditions, yet he'd never had such a reaction to them. He glanced at Taurin, stomach fluttering when he noticed how the light from the open door made his hair shine.

Li glanced around at the work Taurin had done to distract himself from the heat building within him. *I must still be tired*, he told himself. Otherwise, he wouldn't be having such reactions to the one beside him. He didn't even know if Taurin liked *nelim*—males.

Most of the holes around the windows had been patched, and he'd started sanding all the old wood that made up the walls and doors of the stalls. Residual aura and sawdust floated around the space, meaning Taurin had used magic to speed things along—or at least save his hands from all the manual work. He couldn't help but wonder if Taurin had ever done intensive labour like this before. Given how sweaty and red the other elf looked, it didn't seem like it. If he were a fighter of any sort, this activity would have been a breeze. Regardless, Li nodded in approval. Already, the barn was looking much fresher. It had been in a very sorry state when he'd first laid eyes on it at dawn.

"Who built this place?" he asked.

"One of the noble families did," said Taurin through a mouthful of bread. "They had a breeding stable here a long time ago. It was eventually abandoned due to a lack of use. With it being so far from the forest, I think it was too much of a pain to maintain. Some wards still lingered on it when I first arrived, which managed to keep it from falling into complete disrepair. They faded not long after I arrived. A condition of their existence, I guess." He shrugged.

"I suppose that makes sense." Li understood why they didn't want to keep running a stable that was days, if not weeks, away from the forest. "I've nearly finished the roof. I'll come help you in here once I'm done."

"Are you sure you don't want to rest? I can handle things here," said Taurin, worry pinching his brow. "You shouldn't overexert yourself."

Li was a warrior. While mundane work like this was taxing, it wasn't any different from running drills all day. Frequently, they went days without sleep to ensure they could still fight in sub-optimal conditions. Compared to that, fixing the stable after a day of recuperating from being shipwrecked was nothing.

"I'm fine." Li stood up, ready to get back to work. Maybe being outside would help him cool off. "I can't earn my keep if I do nothing all day." He gave Taurin a small smile. As he turned, he swore the other elf's ears turned pink.

The heat in Li's gut turned into a blaze as he hurried outside.

Chapter Five

Ride

"Mmm, she should be alright," said the old, grizzled dwarf. He had Sparrow's bruised hoof cupped in his meaty, wrinkled hand.

Taurin's shoulders slowly relaxed. Good, he didn't think he could handle the stress of dealing with a serious injury. He already had so much on his plate—worries that kept him awake at night.

"Jus' bring her in every night. The damp cold's not great for her. And it's good for her feet to touch somethin' dry," said Grimmst.

"Will do," he said.

Grimmst released Sparrow's hoof and gave her a hearty pat on the shoulder. "She's a tough gal."

"That she is. Thank you for coming out here."

"Bah, it's no problem. Good to leave the farm once in a while. You let me know as soon as any of them look like they're about to foal, ya hear?" Grimmst squinted up at him through thick grey eyebrows that matched his equally thick beard.

"I will. I suspect they'll be ready sometime next moon."

"Good. I know yer learnin' quick, but foalin' ain't somethin' to mess around with. Things can easily go wrong. Don't want them comin' out all twisted." He made a curving motion with his hands.

"I'll make sure to let you know." Taurin gave him an appreciative smile. He heard footsteps approaching and turned to see Li.

"Oh ho! Who's that?" asked Grimmst, wrinkled face scrunched up as he assessed the newcomer.

"You can call me Li." He dipped his head to Grimmst.

"Hmm," hummed the old dwarf, hands on his hips, looking Li up and down. "Never seen an elfie like you before."

"And I've never met a dwarf before."

"Bwah! Well, now you have!" Grimmst gave a hearty laugh.

Taurin let out a breath. He wasn't sure how Grimmst would react to Li, but apparently, he didn't need to worry.

"You're just as willowy looking as the rest. Like a breeze'll snap you in two. Where'd you come from?" asked Grimmst.

Taurin watched Li's face. What would his new helper tell him?

"I washed up on the beach just on the other side of the hills. The sea dumped me there after a storm. I wandered through the hills, and eventually, Taurin found me face down in the pasture."

Grimmst squinted hard at him as if trying to decide whether he believed that tale. "Humph, sea's no place for a dwarf. We sink like rocks. Dense bones and whatnot. You spindly elfies just float."

It was clear Li didn't know what to make of that. Taurin bit back a chuckle. "Alright, I'm going to put Sparrow back in the pasture. Grimmst, do you want a bite to eat before you head out?"

"Naw, I'm good. Have something when I get home." He wandered to the white and brown spotted pony he had hitched to a ring on the barn. "Remember, let me know when they're foalin'. I'll see if I can get Hazel to make some of those flashy magical letters so you can reach me real quick."

"Will do. Thank you Grimmst," said Taurin, untying Sparrow as the dwarf trotted away. Of course, he would make sure Grimmst knew when it was time. He couldn't afford to lose any of the foals—not if he wanted to return to the forest at the end of the summer.

Any mishaps would cost him everything.

Li was looking better each day. Taurin was surprised at how quickly he'd sprung back from being nearly drowned and frozen to death. But each morning after all their chores were done, Li took his sword into the yard and ran drills, determined to keep his skills and body honed. Taurin would sit nearby with Nellie, pull out his leather-bound journal, and sketch the horses. Of course, not much sketching would get done once Li removed his top, finishing his workout with his sweaty, muscled chest exposed. It was hard to stay focused on the horses with a much more intriguing subject in front of him.

"Would you like to learn? I can show you," Li offered, catching Taurin's eye. He held out the enchanted blade, aura thrumming from it.

"No, I'm fine for now," Taurin replied, unable to tear his gaze away from how Li's sweat-slicked muscles stretched and flexed as he swung. The thoughts he kept having about his guest, the sort that made his body react in ways that made it hard to sleep, were best kept to himself.

Maybe one day, if he were really lucky, he wouldn't have to.

"Do you want to go for a ride?" Li asked, sheathing his sword and wiping sweat off his brow. Most of his hair was tied back, a few loose strands framing his face. "I'd like to see the area."

"Sure, let's get cleaned up, and then I can show you around," Taurin said, struggling to keep his tone casual as emotions roiled within him.

He'd managed to find out which sort of partners Li preferred, which, luckily for him, was any gender. "While on longer missions, we'd partner up with each other," Li had explained over breakfast. If he thought it was a strange topic to discuss at the table, he made no mention of it. Now Taurin just needed to know if Li had someone waiting for him back home; he couldn't disrupt an existing relationship. But the thought of asking made his palms sweaty.

After a quick wash, they wrapped up some buns and dried fruit and went to fetch some horses. They led the two stallions out of their pastures, gave them a thorough grooming, then saddled them up.

Li was just as good with horses as he claimed to be; it had become obvious over the past few days. It was a great relief for Taurin—and educational. Just yesterday Li had started instructing him on how to ride bareback.

"It's a good skill to have," Li had said while Oak, one of the geldings, was hitched outside the barn. He had easily mounted the horse without any assistance, placing a hand on Oak's withers and gracefully swinging himself up. Taurin's attempt to mount Oak had been far less elegant. He'd ended up slung over the gelding's back like a sack of vegetables.

"You'll get it," Li had said with an encouraging smile that had made Taurin's heart skip a beat.

As they rode along the dirt road, Taurin debated taking them east into the hills, then thought better of it. Li had had a rough few days in there. Instead he took them west into the prairie, wanting to show him something new.

The ground beneath the tall grasses was drier than the field back home, not being constantly churned up by the daily movement of animals. Most of the grass was still brown, but some of it was starting to turn gold again. Taurin kept them on the dirt road, not wanting to risk one of the stallions stepping in an unseen hole. A broken leg was beyond his ability to heal.

"Do you have places like this back home?" he asked.

Li stared out at the open expanse of grass that stretched beyond what the eye could see. "Similar, though I don't think it's quite as large. Usually you can see mountains in the distance, but here I see nothing."

"The Sky Peak Mountains on the far side are days, if not weeks, away."

"I didn't see them on the map," said Li, looking around to see if he could spot anything else besides rolling prairie.

"No, my map only shows half the area. The Manwan Plains extend beyond, eventually turning into the mountains. We're right on the eastern edge of the plains. They stretch further east to west than north to south. The heart of the prairie is a very different beast," explained Taurin.

"Have you been there?"

He shook his head. "No, there isn't much there aside from dragons. The dwarves seem to like it, though. They've got a city and some villages out there. We elves prefer to stick closer to the forests, or the rivers."

"Dragons?"

"Yeah, they like to hunt the *nuu*. Large, hairy, hooved beasts," he explained upon seeing Li's questioning glance. "They live in massive herds all over the prairie. A dragon will swoop down at a herd, causing them to run, then use their fire and talons to try to isolate one. It's pretty dangerous, because if they lose control and fall, they can get crushed by the stampede."

"Lovely," said Li, crinkling his nose in a way that had Taurin's chest fluttering. "Do they come this far east?"

"Not that I'm aware of. I rarely see nuu, never mind dragons. They have no reason to venture this far. It's a long way from their home in the Sky Peak Mountains."

"So you're not worried about your horses being attacked?" Li asked.

"Not at all." Taurin gazed up at the clear blue sky. Summer was on its way. Hopefully the heat would help dry the pasture. He didn't want to have to raise foals in the muck. A few sunny days would do wonders. "My wards only extend to terrestrial threats, not sky-borne ones."

Li hummed.

"What?" asked Taurin.

"I think you should add wards, just in case."

Taurin regarded him for a moment, marvelling at how the sun shone on his pitch black hair. It was like the most rich and luxurious of inks. He wanted to run his hands through it. Was it as silky as it looked? He quickly looked back at the road, the tips of his ears itching. "I'll think about it." He didn't have the ability to cast wards like that, nor the resources to hire someone.

"If I may be so bold," said Li, "why are you running the stable? You're new to caring for horses, and no one aside from the dwarves is around to help."

Taurin's hand tightened around the reins. "I needed to get away from the city. To try something new. I'm not very old, only partway through my second century." The lie he'd come up with a few days ago came easily to him. He couldn't tell Li the truth—the warrior would surely leave if he did. And Taurin didn't want to have to go back to tending to the horses alone. Especially not with foaling season so close.

Li looked at him. Taurin didn't meet his dark eyes, fearing he'd spill if he did.

"I suppose that's not unreasonable," Li said after a moment. "You come from a noble family I presume?"

"Yes." Taurin's grip relaxed, glad the topic had changed, though he suspected Li didn't fully believe him. "My family name is Dusktrail. We're somewhat influential in Lyrellis." Powerful enough that he'd been offered the opportunity to try getting the breeding stable off the ground. Because the alternative was far less desirable.

They came to a fork in the road and halted their mounts.

"That northern path leads to Greenwind, the nearest dwarven town, and eventually up to the forest that holds Sylandris," explained Taurin. "The other takes us west, deeper into the prairie."

"I'd like to see Greenwind," said Li, eyes wandering along the worn path. Countless hooves and carts had tamped it down flat despite the spring melt.

Taurin hadn't anticipated that journey. "It's too far to go today. We can plan a trip another time." Maybe he could take Matil up on her offer for lunch.

If Li was disappointed, he didn't show it. He simply nodded.

Taurin rubbed the top of his ear, feeling like he'd let his companion down. He signalled King to keep moving along the western road. "What about your family?"

"I come from a well-known clan of warriors. We've served the empire for generations."

That was easy to see. Even in the saddle, Li had the air of nobility. His posture was perfect, and his dark brown stallion, Par-Par, listened to him without hesitation, despite it being their first ride. Normally, it took a while for a horse to warm up to a new rider. Li had clearly lived a highly disciplined life.

"Once you're feeling better, do you plan on returning home?" Taurin asked, fidgeting with his reins in a way that made King flick an ear at him. He needed to know.

"I have no desire to return to the empire," said Li slowly.

Taurin blinked. *Really?* With how Li carried himself and continued to practice with his sword every day, Taurin expected him to want to go back.

Tension slowly melted out of him. Li wasn't leaving. And if he wasn't leaving, it meant no one was waiting for him back across the sea. Maybe he could... "Well, you're welcome to stay with me as long as you want."

"Thank you." Li dipped his head.

They rode for a while longer. Taurin told him what it was like to grow up in the royal city of Lyrellis, and about all the lessons he'd taken as a *thelim*—a child. "We're exposed to a variety of subjects and arts to see what sticks with us. If someone proves to be skilled with both magic and sword, then there's a good chance they will opt to join the Elithar once they're an adult. They're the royal guard in charge of protecting not just the royal family but all of Sylandris. They're warriors like you."

"So, you get to choose what you pursue when you're older?" asked Li, curious.

"Yes. Is it not the same for you?"

"No, whatever skills we show promise in are the skills we are made to hone. Someone who prefers to use the sword but is skilled in magic will be told to hone their magical abilities."

Taurin frowned. "But what if you don't like doing the thing you're most skilled at?"

Li shook his head. "What we want is not important. It's about how we can best serve the Cloud Empire. The empire is only as strong as its weakest citizens."

Taurin understood what he was saying, but it didn't seem fair. The empire may be strong, but was it happy? He supposed not if Li didn't want to go back despite serving them for decades. *I wonder what happened to make him unwilling to return?* It wasn't a question Taurin felt comfortable asking.

"Let's stop here for a break."

Moving to the side of the road, they dismounted. They gave the horses some water from the skins tied to their saddles, then laid out a woven blanket on the grass. Taurin produced some buns and dried fruit from one of the saddlebags.

"Sorry if they're a bit stale," he said, handing Li a bun.

Li settled himself on the colourful blanket. "I'm sure they're fine. Aren't you worried about the horses running off?" They weren't tethered to anything.

Taurin sat on the blanket beside him. "No, and if they did, they'd likely just run back home." The stallions in question were busy pushing their noses through the tall grass, looking for sweet new spring shoots to eat.

They ate the buns, which weren't as stale as Taurin feared, and nibbled on the strips of fruit.

Due to the swishing grass, they couldn't see much around them, so they turned their gaze to the sky. It was a brilliant blue today, with only a few clouds lazily drifting by. A nice reprieve from the grey of winter. A flock of birds flew by far overhead, reminding them that summer was on its way.

Taurin pulled out his journal, and started sketching with a stick of charcoal.

"What are you drawing?" asked Li, trying to peer at the book.

"Just the prairie," he replied, detailing the seedpod on a stalk of grass. He wanted to draw more than that, but not when the subject he wanted to capture was watching him.

Li watched him briefly before returning his gaze to the land around them. "It's quiet out here."

"Mm, it certainly is." Taurin spared a glance towards his companion, then looked down, noticing that Li's hand was close to his leg. A thought suddenly consumed him. What if... He lowered the hand holding the charcoal right as Li shifted positions, moving his out of reach.

Taurin quickly redirected his hand to the journal. He breathed in deeply, the smell of fresh earth and horse clearing his head. His gaze returned to the sky. "It's nice and relaxing, nothing like the chaos of Lyrellis."

"Definitely better than being tossed around on a boat for who knows how long," said Li. He leaned back, arms stretched out behind him with his hands planted on the ground to brace himself.

Taurin grasped the opportunity. Heart racing, he set aside his journal and copied Li. As he got into position, their hands touched. Instantly, his ears began to itch. Was he being too bold? Yet to his relief, Li didn't pull away.

"I'm glad we came out here," said Li.

Taurin's eyes flicked to his companion. A jolt shot through him when he realized that Li was looking at him with his black eyes. No, not black. A rich, dark brown. "So am I," Taurin said, fighting to keep his voice even.

Li was suddenly close. Too close. His face was right in front of him. Taurin could count every one of his long eyelashes. Li's lips parted, still chapped from his time at sea. But Taurin didn't care. Heart threatening to burst out of his chest, he leaned in, mouth opening to meet Li's.

His lips were warm and surprisingly soft. Clearly, the wax salve Taurin had given him was working. Heat surged through, unrelated to the sunlight warming the earth around them. A hand gently ran through his hair. Taurin's heart skipped a beat, his stomach fluttering at the contact. In turn, he pressed a hand to Li's cheek, cupping it gently, wanting more of the warrior before him. His fingers moved from Li's cheek to his hair, every bit as soft as Taurin had fantasized, like the most luxurious spider silks the royal family wore.

A hot tongue pushed between his lips, and Taurin eagerly accepted it, catching hints of sweetness from the berries mixed with Li's own flavour. It was intoxicating.

And Taurin was hungry for more.

Chapter Six

Language

They rode in silence.

Li thought of nothing but the kiss the entire ride back. And judging by Taurin's bright red ears, he was doing the same.

He'd been so worried that Taurin would reject his advance, but now he was glad he'd gone for it. The empire preferred that elves take partners of another gender, wanting their population to grow. But they didn't enforce this on active warriors. Until they retired from service, they could be with whomever they pleased so long as it didn't hinder their ability to serve. Still, it caused some to hesitate to take partners they couldn't eventually reproduce with.

The kiss had been a risk. One that could have led to Taurin kicking him out, leaving him completely alone again in this strange land. Going off the fact that Taurin had casually asked him about his preferences, he suspected it was safe to try. And it had paid off. Something new had been born between them. Or so he hoped.

Taurin hadn't shied away. He'd accepted Li's mouth, their tongues entwining, discovering each other. Taurin tasted sweet, though how much of that was from the dried fruit they'd been eating, Li couldn't say. They'd have to do it again sometime.

Li had wanted to see how much further they could go, but the snorting of the horses had brought them back to reality; a wagon was approaching down the road. They had hastily broken apart, trying to look casual.

"Dwarven eyes aren't as farseeing as ours," Taurin had told him. Li prayed it was true. At least the tall grass helped to hide them.

Despite Taurin's receptiveness, doubt started to creep in as they rode. Li worried his past would catch up to him, even though the ocean separated them. He liked the stable, and feared what would happen if blue-clad warriors marched up the road one day. He and Taurin didn't stand a chance against them. And out here on the prairie there was no one around to help them.

Par-Par stumbled as he stepped in a hole, jolting him in the saddle. "Easy there," Li said, petting his steed's soft neck. His hand came away covered in fur; they were still shedding their winter coats despite his and Taurin's best efforts to groom them. Par-Par continued like nothing had happened.

"Are you two alright?" Taurin asked.

"We're fine. I should have been more attentive."

"Well, we're nearly home."

The ride back seemed both longer and shorter than the ride out. Li had initially wondered if they would be able to pick up where they had left off once they returned, but the mood had passed.

The stable soon came into view. Though Liander had only been there for a few days, the familiar sight of the barn, the pasture, and the cottage on the hill, was comforting. No, he would never let anyone from his homeland ruin this.

But that means I must leave this place.

He stiffened up as he dismounted, nearly landing on his ass.

"Li!"

"All good, just caught my foot in the stirrup," he said, face hot. He'd never fallen off a horse before! *Get a hold of yourself.*

He would only have to leave if there was any hint that someone had followed him, and given the storm, there was no way anyone would suspect he was alive...nothing had washed up on the beach with him. No one knew he was here, save for Taurin and the dwarves. None of them would rat him out. He doubted they had any way of contacting the empire. Taurin certainly didn't; he'd never even heard of it before. And he'd never seen any dwarves back across the sea.

I'm safe, he repeated like a mantra.

Now, if only he could believe it.

"Here, let me show you a better way," Li said a few mornings later. They were out in the pasture, trying to catch one of the mares to give her a health check. Taurin liked to examine them twice a moon: once himself and once with Grimmst or one of his apprentices.

Quill, the pregnant red roan mare in question wouldn't come near them.

"She doesn't like the exam. I don't know why. Nothing bad has happened to her that I know of."

"Perhaps it's from her previous owner." A breeze ruffled Li's long, dark hair, its bite no longer as cold as it had been when he'd first shown up.

"Must be," replied Taurin.

"Yet she has no issue with you bringing her carrots in the morning."

"No, it's only when she sees the halter." Taurin clutched it behind his back, trying to hide it from view. Yet Quill eyed them suspiciously from where she stood with a few others.

"Since she knows we're up to something, trying to go to her isn't going to work," explained Li. "We have to convince her to come to us."

"I've tried treats in the past. It only worked the first few times." He crossed his arms.

"They're smarter than that. And quick learners," Li smirked.

"They sure are," Taurin sighed. "What's your plan?"

"Contrary to what I just said, we'll approach her, but not directly."

"Do you mind if I stand back and watch? Two of us might spook her."

Li nodded and took the woven rope halter from him. "Pay close attention to our body language."

Calmly, he started towards Quill. He didn't walk directly at her, but in the general direction of the group of mares. Quill didn't move away until he was within a few paces. He followed in her footsteps, knowing it was making her uncomfortable to have him in her blind spot. When she turned her head to look at him, he stopped and took a step back, turning his body away from her, rewarding the behaviour and lessening the pressure. When she started moving again, so did he, only backing away when she exhibited behaviour he wanted to reinforce. He made sure to keep his body language relaxed: a cocked knee when he was still, his body never squared towards her.

They kept up this dance for a while. Li knew the key was to be persistent but patient. Rushing things would only startle her and blow any ounce of trust he'd earned so far. Quill started looking at him more, picking up on his consistent reactions. When she stopped again, he felt confident to start approaching, moving towards her rear in a non-threatening manner. She kept her eye on him, moving again once he got too close.

The next time Quill stopped, he was able to get nearer, still moving towards her rump instead of her head. She turned to look at him but didn't move. Li held out his empty hand, wanting her to initiate the contact to build her confidence. She pressed her muzzle to it, sniffing him. Pleased with the result, Li gently petted her back, not trying to get the halter on her just yet. Her ears were still pinned back on her head, the most obvious sign that she was tense.

He paused his petting and held out his hand; she touched it again. He repeated the cycle of petting and letting her touch him a few times before holding up the halter. Like his hand, he wanted her to touch it of her own volition. Li offered it to her a few times before she would press her nose to it. Once she did, he touched it to her body—not her face. He rubbed it along her side, mimicking the petting motion from earlier.

Once Quill started to lick her lips and chew, turning her head to touch the halter before he'd offer it up, he knew it was time. Li gently draped the lead rope over the base of her neck, taking it slow. He held the halter out, and when she touched it, he gently slid it over her muzzle and ears, then fastened it shut.

"Good girl," he murmured, patting her neck and giving her a piece of dried fruit from his pocket.

Li led her over to Taurin, who was staring at him with wonder.

"You did it! I'm impressed," said the golden elf.

"Do you understand what I did?" *Impressed that I could catch her, or impressed with something else?* He occasionally caught Taurin staring at him with a particular and distracting gleam in his eye. It took all his focus to pretend he hadn't noticed.

Why did being around Taurin cause decades of careful training to unravel?

"I think so. I'll give it a try next time." Taurin accepted the lead rope from Li, and they walked Quill up to the barn.

Once Quill was tied in place, Li watched as Taurin ran his hands over her, checking for any lumps, bumps, cuts, or otherwise tender areas. He crossed his arms and leaned against the wooden barn, fighting to keep his face neutral. Gods, how he wished Taurin's hands were on him instead. Maybe...maybe later.

They hadn't done anything since their kiss a few days ago. Taurin hadn't brought it up. Had he not liked it? He'd seemed to in the moment. Though Li had previously slept with some of the other warriors, nothing had been serious. He hadn't been in an intimate emotional relationship with them, at least not in the romantic sense. It had simply been a way to relieve stress. But what he felt towards Taurin was different. He didn't fully understand it yet, but right now, he was getting jealous over a horse. And that was a sign that *something* was up. Was it love? Perhaps. He'd never been romantically interested in anyone before.

And now isn't the time to start. He crossed his arms over his chest, brow furrowed. His days at the stable were ticking down. Sooner or later, he would have to leave. His heart twinged painfully at the thought. There was no point in pursuing what he was feeling. It would only make things harder in the end.

Yet as Taurin checked Quill over, Li's dark eyes watched the back of Taurin's hands move and flex. He couldn't push away the thoughts of those soft hands trailing down his back, his chest, going lower to touch other places. He suppressed a shiver.

Damn it. Normally, he was able to stamp down desire. Douse it like a bucket of water on a fire. It was a basic skill all warriors had to perfect: show no weakness, leave nothing to exploit. Well, right now, Li was failing miserably. His captain would be livid, but he didn't care. Taurin had already seen him at his weakest, passed out in the pasture.

Maybe he'd lost more in the shipwreck than he thought. Being tossed about the waves could have rattled his tightly bound emotions loose. Or maybe that came with being in a strange place where he had nothing to worry about.

Except for being found.

"Li," Taurin said, pulling him from the depths of his self-analysis. By the way Taurin looked at him, he must have called his name a few times.

"Sorry. What is it?"

"Is everything alright?" There was a concerned look on his face.

"I was just thinking about the empire."

Taurin's expression softened. "I understand."

Guilt burned in his stomach. Taurin believed him to be a simple castaway, but there was more to the story than that. But Li didn't think it would be wise to share. Not yet. Not until he knew it was safe. And he didn't know how Taurin would take the revelation. Still, he didn't like hiding it. Taurin had been nothing but kind to him; it felt wrong to keep things from him, especially something as important as this.

Once I know whether or not the empire is after me, I will tell him.

Assuming he was still around to do so.

Chapter Seven

Epiphany

The last dregs of snow finally melted as the days grew warmer. The pasture was muddy near the barn, but it was drying up farther out. Nights were still cool, so Taurin continued to bring the pregnant mares indoors to sleep. To his relief, Sparrow's bruised hoof seemed to have healed; she was walking and running normally again. He let her stay out with the others overnight.

Judging by how big their bellies were, he suspected the four mares would be ready to foal within the moon. Maybe sooner. He and Li were working hard to make sure everything was ready for when the time came. He'd never seen a horse—or anything—give birth before, but Li and the dwarves had educated him on what to look out for.

"There will be obvious signs, but sometimes they don't start until the middle of the night," Li explained over a quick breakfast of eggs and tea.

Nellie pecked at the floor under the table, eating whatever they dropped. She now followed them to the house each evening instead of sleeping in the coop.

"Then I guess I'll be staying awake all night," said Taurin.

"Once they're closer to their due dates, we'll set up a watch," Li said, "You can't stay up for days on end just in case one of them goes into labour. We'll take turns."

"Mmm, I suppose you're right." He hadn't really thought about that.

"Are you able to weave a spell that could alert us?"

As Li sipped his tea, Taurin tried not to look at the lips he longed to kiss again but was afraid to. Had the kiss on the prairie been a one-time thing? Li hadn't initiated anything else since…

"I've—I've been trying," he stammered, "but haven't been able to come up with anything that will work. It's not like the wards I've cast on the pasture, which trigger anytime anything touches them. Detecting a horse going into labour takes a certain type of finesse I don't possess."

"I don't think I would be able to do it either," said the warrior. "Most of the magic I've learned is for combat. Is there anyone in Lyrellis you could ask?"

"Not that I would be comfortable asking." There were a few elves he suspected could do it, but they certainly wouldn't be open to helping him. Not after what had happened in the city. Besides, he wasn't allowed visitors from the forest. "Come,"

Taurin said, standing up and taking their plates, "let's go groom the herd."

"Who are the sires?" Li asked as they stood in the pasture, brushing muck off the mares. Taurin couldn't wait to be free of mud season. Sure, summer rains would make things messy, but they didn't fall as frequently as in the spring.

"King was bred to Han-Han, and Par-Par to Breeze and Quill. Han-Han and Par-Par have lineages that hail from the royal stable. They're not related, but I wanted to mix them with new blood instead of breeding them to each other. King was a gift from my parents, and the dwarves helped me find Breeze."

"And what about Lily? She's a gorgeous horse."

"She also hails from a bloodline back home."

"And who did you breed her to? King as well?"

Taurin fought to get a stubborn bit of mud out of Lily's dappled coat, not sure how to answer the question. "No, not King. Nor Par-Par."

"So you got a breeding contract with someone?"

"Not exactly."

"Alright," said Li, clearly not satisfied with the non-answer but not digging into it.

The truth was that Taurin wasn't sure who the stallion was. He hadn't been able to find a good match for her noble bloodline, thus hadn't bred her. Yet he'd noticed her getting bigger over the winter. Grimmst had come over to confirm the pregnancy. Taurin was certain his stallions weren't the culprit; his wards would have alerted him to them entering the mares' paddock. But they hadn't been tripped by anything. Not even a wild animal.

Now, he had his suspicion as to the sire, but he felt silly voicing it. Or rather, he worried that speaking it would jinx it, and Lily would lose her foal. And Taurin couldn't afford that. If the sire was who he believed it to be, then Lily's foal would be worth a fortune. He would be allowed to return home.

The horse in question turned her head to nip at him.

"Hey!" he exclaimed, pulling his arm out of the way.

"Rub her udder. Mares like it," said Li.

"Her udder?" he asked incredulously.

"Yes."

Taurin stared at Lily.

"Do you not know where it is?" asked Li, a hint of amusement in his voice.

"I know where it is," Taurin huffed indignantly.

"Do you want me to show you?" Li was suddenly beside him. "Give me your hand." He held out his.

Taurin's heart skipped a beat, mind blanking. Trying to hide his hesitation, he let Li take it. He prayed that Li couldn't feel how hot his skin had suddenly become.

"Here. Just be gentle." He placed Taurin's hand under Lily's large belly between her rear legs.

Trying to calm his racing pulse, he gently rubbed the area, guided by Li. Lily grunted and shifted her weight, relaxing.

"What do you know..." said Taurin.

"Most mares enjoy it, especially the ones with foal."

"You really understand them."

"Like I mentioned before, I've spent a lot of time with horses. I pretty much lived in the saddle back home. We had to know how to care for our mounts when we went out on missions." Li dropped his hand and moved away to start grooming Quill.

Taurin felt a pang of...disappointment? Loss?

"Right." That made sense. If they were out in the middle of nowhere and one got hurt, the warriors needed to know how to care for them. "What kind of missions?"

"Mostly patrols, but sometimes we would aid villages that were being plagued by fell beasts or bandits."

"Bandits?" Bandits were unheard of in these lands. At least, in those the elves controlled. He wasn't too sure about the dwarves.

"The Cloud Empire may be led by elven nobles, but humans live there as well. It's a massive expanse of land. It can take moons to ride from end to end."

Taurin couldn't imagine it, but he'd never left the forest until now. Even then, the Sky Peak Mountains to the west were less than a moon's ride away. "I'd be interested in seeing it one day."

Li kept grooming Quill, silent.

"Should the opportunity arise," Taurin added hastily.

"It's not as great as it sounds. Bandits, remember?"

"I think I can handle myself against a couple of human bandits." Humans didn't live in Sylandris, but their boats occasionally came up along the Greenstone River, passing through the region to reach the sea or the north-western lands.

"Not all of them are human."

Taurin blinked. Why would elves feel the need to stoop to something like that? Sure, elves stole, but he'd never heard of anyone taking up true banditry. "Why—"

"I don't know what it's like in Lyrellis or your other cities, but things are complicated back home. Not everyone is happy with how the imperial family runs things. And that leads to a lot of in-fighting, and families being torn apart. Some end up with nothing and must do whatever they can to survive." He moved to a golden horse with a cream mane and tail.

Taurin frowned. Li's tone was even, but it made him wonder if Li was one of those unhappy with the imperial family. That would explain why he'd been sailing across the ocean—and why he didn't want to go back.

"That's very unfortunate," Taurin said. "It's a ruler's job to make sure their people are content and flourishing." He finished grooming Quill and started brushing another mare.

"Different rulers have different ideas of what a 'flourishing' nation looks like."

Ah. Perhaps it was time to drop the topic.

"Sun there seems to like you," he said, watching Li brush dried dirt off the palomino's flank.

"She's a lovely shade of gold."

"You should ride her next time we go out. I think she'd like that."

Sun bobbed her head.

"See?"

"I suppose I can't say no to a lovely lady," said Li, a faint smile on his lips.

Taurin's heart fluttered. If only Li would look at him like that.

Then it suddenly hit him. Li wasn't doing anything because he hadn't responded after the kiss. *By the gods, he probably thinks I'm not interested! I'm a fool.*

Well, Taurin would make sure he knew.

"Li, I..." The words died on his lips as Li turned towards him, nerves fleeing at the sight of his handsome face. *Fuck.* This wasn't going to be easy.

"Do you need help with something?" He was already finished grooming Sun. The mare had been the cleanest of the bunch when they'd started.

Flustered, Taurin opened and closed his mouth a few times. "I, do you—the ride..." His face burned.

Li tilted his head. "...what?"

Taurin wished he could disappear. He took a deep breath. Instead of speaking, he stepped around Lily, closing the space between them.

The mood shifted.

Taurin's heart thudded against his ribs. Li was so close—too close. Taurin wanted to step back, yet he pushed himself forward. Trembling, he closed his eyes, unable to meet Li's gaze. Lips brushed; his mouth parted. Strong arms pulled their bodies together.

Taurin melted as heat rushed through him. He wrapped his arms around Li, holding him close as their lips met. He could taste their shared breath, mixed with hints of the tea they'd had at breakfast. Hands ran up and down along his back, feeling him through his clothes. He returned the favour but was immediately frustrated by all the fabric between them. Li was wearing entirely too many layers!

Apparently, his partner felt the same way; a hand had slipped under his tunic. His skin prickled at the touch; Li's hand was covered in fur.

Still, Taurin groaned as Li explored the planes of his back and heat pooled in his groin. Shit. Taurin resisted the urge to grind against Li like an animal in heat. That was excruciatingly difficult; it had been far too long since he'd been with anyone, and his body craved attention. But he was afraid of rushing things. Though his last relationship had ended a while ago, it hadn't ended well.

Li settled his hands on Taurin's hips and broke the kiss. They stood there, panting like winded horses.

Taurin felt very exposed as Li stared into his eyes, losing himself in their rich darkness.

"Do you want to keep going?" Li asked quietly, as if worried someone would hear. Yet he pulled Taurin's hips against his, and Taurin was suddenly very aware of Li's own need.

They needed to get inside. Now.

"The b-barn is closest," Taurin stammered. "If you're fine wi—"

Face flushed, Li grabbed his hand and all but dragged him there, shutting the door behind them. With a flick of the wrist, all the windows blew shut, plunging them into darkness. With another, he lit the lanterns; they gave off an intimate red glow.

Taurin's heart raced with anticipation. He quickly threw a horse blanket into one of the clean box stalls. Then Li was upon him.

Their lips crashed together again.

This wasn't how Taurin had imagined their first time would be, but he didn't care. He snaked a hand into Li's top, roaming over his chest. Li's toned muscles flexed with each breath he took.

Li's hands ran down his back to his soft ass, giving it a squeeze and causing Taurin to grind against him, moaning faintly into the kiss. Li manoeuvred him down onto the blanket, their lips firmly locked together.

Laying on his back, Taurin finally ended the kiss. He snapped his fingers, and a vial appeared in his hand. "Use this," he said in a breathy voice. He was glad the light hid how red his cheeks were.

Li straddled him on his knees, setting the vial aside.

Taurin, looking up at Li, shuddered. The light cast strange shadows across his face, accentuating his sharp features and making his eyes seem even darker. Gods, he was *gorgeous*.

Li ducked down and gently kissed his cheek. His hands got to work on Taurin's pants, pulling them down to expose his desire. Taurin shivered as cool air hit him, though it wouldn't be cold for long. Reaching up, he rubbed Li's length through the fabric that kept it bound.

Li's breath hitched.

Taurin undid the ties holding up Li's pants and let them fall, revealing what was hidden inside.

"You're sure?" Li asked, voice husky.

"Absolutely," Taurin breathed.

They hastily kicked off their boots and pulled off the rest of their garments.

"You have a tattoo," said Li, running a finger over the brown mark over Taurin's heart. It was shaped sort of like a gentle wave, with thin filigree-like curls branching from it.

Taurin shivered. "Don't you have one? All elves are marked once they reach adulthood." Yet he couldn't see one anywhere on his partner.

"No. We're advised against receiving tattoos or marks. They're too easily recognizable."

Taurin supposed that made sense, but it felt odd. The mark was a symbol of maturity. A symbol of acceptance and belonging. Each one was different, unique to the elf.

Li scooped up the vial and poured a generous amount of the viscous liquid onto his fingers.

Taurin, trembling with anticipation, lifted and spread his pale legs, exposing himself. He saw Li swallow as his partner repositioned himself between them. Eyes hooded, Li pressed a slicked finger to him.

Taurin bit his lip as Li eased it in. There was very little pain. Though Taurin hadn't been with a partner in a while, that didn't mean he hadn't found other ways to deal with his body's needs.

"Tell me if you want me to stop," Li said, voice low but insistent.

"Keep going," said Taurin with no hesitation.

Li stroked his cheek with his other hand. Taurin leaned into the touch.

One by one, Li added more fingers, stretching and spreading him. Taurin writhed on the blanket, biting back mewls of pleasure.

Then suddenly, he felt very empty.

Li uncorked the vial and poured the rest on his member.

"Wait," said Taurin, "let me." Sitting up, he reached out and grasped Li's warmth.

The other elf stiffened as Taurin stroked him, coating the entire thing with oil. Li stared at him with an intensity that Taurin felt to the core of his being—a look like that could push him over the edge.

As he lay back down, he sensually licked oil off his elegant fingers, lips glistening in the flickering light.

Li made a needy sound in his throat and positioned himself against Taurin's entrance. Taurin grasped at the blanket as pulsing heat slowly spread him.

"Li..." he murmured, voice dripping with need.

"Patience..." Li sounded like he was barely hanging on. But he gave Taurin time to adjust before slowly starting to move.

The sound of their gentle lovemaking filled the barn, needy cries and pleasured moans echoing throughout. Taurin wrapped his legs around Li, keeping him close. They kissed again and again, lips red and swollen. Neither of them cared as they sought new heights of ecstasy.

Taurin's worries and stresses melted away, the outside world ceasing to exist as their bodies became one. He touched Li's cheek. This was all that mattered.

Stars burst behind Taurin's closed eyes when Li hit that sweet spot deep inside him. His entire body tightened just before his mind went blank as they were pushed over the edge. His legs tightened around Li, crying out as pleasure swept through him like a wave.

His strength fled, his mind left floating among the clouds. A great weight pressed down on him. Li. Taurin wrapped his arms around the spent warrior lying on top of him.

"How was it?" Li asked. It was hard to read his tone.

"Fantastic," he murmured. "I didn't realize how much I needed that." Li was nothing like his previous partner who had treated Taurin's pleasure as an afterthought.

Li rolled off him and pulled him close, nuzzling the crook of his neck. "Neither did I."

Taurin smiled softly. "Then let this not be the only time."

A pause.

"Of course," replied Li, voice gravelly.

Still flushed, both elves remained on the blanket until their shared panting slowed.

"I suppose we have to get up," said Taurin. Though it had worked in the heat of the moment, the blanket wasn't too comfortable. Straw poked his bare skin.

"Soon. Just a moment longer."

Playing with a silky strand of Li's hair, Taurin obliged.

Chapter Eight

Storm

What was I thinking?

It was a gloomy morning; the grey sky threatened rain at any moment. It perfectly reflected Li's dour mood. He'd turned out the pregnant mares while Taurin prepared breakfast and was now feeding the stallions handfuls of berries.

All he could think about was their romp in the hay yesterday—though the high of their activities had since worn off, leaving him with a twisted heart. He liked Taurin, there was no doubt about that, but that's why today's guilt hit so hard.

If he wanted to keep Taurin safe, he would have to leave this place soon. Sleeping with him was only making it harder. *I shouldn't have done it.* Normally, Li could keep himself in check, but something about Taurin dissolved his restraint faster than a bursting dam.

Things couldn't go on like this. The sooner he left, the better. But his heart ached at the thought.

Taurin wasn't like the warriors he'd slept with back home. There was a genuine connection between them, a spark. But Li couldn't let himself be drawn to the light. Not if he wanted that light to continue shining.

If anyone from across the sea showed up...he didn't want to think about it. Perhaps his original offer to stay and help had been a mistake.

Par-Par snorted and nosed him, looking for more fruit.

"Yes, here you go," he said to the cranky liver chestnut stallion, feeding him another slice. He scratched the horse's neck, lost in thought.

It was important to put as much distance between himself and the farm as possible. He could run, but he was better off getting a mount. Unfortunately, he had no money, which meant he would have to steal one of Taurin's horses. The thought made him sick. He couldn't do that to Taurin; leaving was bad enough.

He heard Taurin calling him and returned to the house for breakfast. Par-Par snorted irritably as he left, as if judging him for his horse-thieving thoughts.

"How often do you get news from home?" Li asked as they sat at the wooden kitchen table.

Taurin sipped his tea. "Not too frequently," he said slowly. "Why?"

"Just curious." Guilt gnawed at him. He wondered if perhaps someone from the Cloud Empire had gone to Sylandris. "They would inform you if something important happened, right?"

Taurin furrowed his brow and set down his cup. "Has something happened?"

"No, nothing that I know of." He wouldn't met Taurin's eyes.

"I hope they would send word, but I'm not that important. I may be part of a noble family, but sending a messenger all the way out here isn't worth anyone's time."

Li picked at his food. If someone had gone to Sylandris, then he wouldn't know until they came knocking. *But why would they think to check here? They have no reason to. The storm obliterated everything.*

With that thought, he relaxed. Maybe he didn't have to leave right away. He picked up his mug of tea, letting it warm his hands for a moment before taking a sip.

"This is a nice blend."

"Thank you. The base is a dark one the dwarves like, but I added some of my favourite flowers to give it a lighter flavour."

"I think you were successful."

Taurin smiled. "And I think you need your own bed. Sleeping on the couch all the time can't be that comfortable."

Li blinked, caught off guard by the change in topic. "I really don't mind it. Nellie keeps me company every night." Where would they put another bed? There was no space down here, and the bedroom upstairs was an open loft.

Taurin seemed to read his mind. "There's lots of space upstairs. We can put up a wall if you want."

Sleep upstairs with Taurin? He felt conflicted. Down here he wasn't intruding. But up there, even with some sort of divider, they would share the same space. It felt rather intimate.

"I feel bad making you sleep down here," said Taurin. "There's enough scrap wood leftover from repairing the barn to build a bed frame."

Meeting Taurin's excited expression, it was hard to say no. There was no real reason to say no, besides Li's own swirling emotions. "Then I suppose that's our next task—though the wall is unnecessary."

A flash illuminated the room, followed by a loud crack of thunder. The wind suddenly picked up, howling against the house. Rain splattered the windows.

Taurin glanced out the window and leapt to his feet. "We need to get the mares back in."

Throwing on their coats, they hurried outside, all thoughts of the bed forgotten.

The wind nearly blew them off their feet as they hurried down the hill. Rain fell sideways, stinging their faces.

"Hurry!" Taurin called, panic evident in his voice.

Lightning flashed, blinding them. A deafening clap of thunder shook the ground. Panicked horses screamed and the orange cat shot across the yard towards the barn. The air took on a strange burning smell.

"No!" Taurin shouted.

Blinking away spots, Li squinted through the rain. Partway down one side, lightning had struck the fence, burning away the wards and leaving a charred hole.

The mares snorted and stomped, huddled together near the section of fence that split them from the stallions.

Taurin made an opening, and the two of them darted through. "Catch the pregnant ones first!"

Li didn't need to be told.

Lead ropes in hand, they slowly approached the frightened herd. They couldn't risk causing a stampede.

Sliding on the muddy ground, they caught the pregnant mares one by one and took them into the barn. The rest they moved into the stallions' paddocks. There weren't enough stalls for everyone.

Li unclipped the last lead rope.

"Did you catch Quill?" asked Taurin.

Li turned. "No, I thought you had her?"

Horror crept over Taurin's face. They bolted to the barn. The red mare wasn't there.

Shit.

Li swept past Taurin, heart clenching at the distraught look on the golden elf's face. He quickly caught Par-Par from the field and threw a bridle on him, not wasting time with a saddle. "I'll look for her, you dry off the others!" He guided Par-Par to the charred hole. As he feared, hoof prints went from the hole to the open prairie beyond.

"Come on, boy!" Li wheeled Par-Par around, glad the cranky stallion wasn't fazed by the storm, and followed the tracks.

They were nearly impossible to follow in the storm, and he had to keep Par-Par at a slow lope so as not to lose them. For once, the muddy ground had its use. Li didn't know how long they rode, but it reminded him of his awful days in the hills. At least this time, he had a place to return to.

For now.

He pushed those thoughts away. He could worry about his own situation once they'd found Quill. He reached out with his aura, trying to sense the more. But horses didn't have damai, so he couldn't feel a thing. He had to rely on his mundane senses.

Par-Par's ears twitched.

"Do you hear something? Is it Quill?"

Stallions watched over their herds. Maybe he could find the missing mare.

Li gave him more rein, letting him pick the way.

The rain started to ease up as he rode, but the wind continued to howl, chilling him. He kept a careful eye on the muddy prints, only redirecting Par-Par when he believed the horse had strayed from Quill's path.

Par-Par's ears remained pricked forward. He suddenly stopped and let out a loud neigh.

Li was still on his back, the shrill call piercing his ears. "You calling her?" he said quietly.

The stallion flicked an ear, then took off at a bouncy trot. Had Li been a lesser rider, he would've fallen. All warriors were trained to ride bareback in case of an emergency, something he was determined for Taurin to learn. Taurin was progressing slowly but surely. He could get on and off without help and could ride at a comfortable walk.

Par-Par trumpeted again, transitioning to a canter.

In the distance, Li heard a response.

The stallion broke into a gallop. Li crouched low, making no effort to slow him. He focused on moving with his steed's rhythm as Par-Par's legs stretched and curled. Grass flew by in a blur as they raced past.

No wonder he bred Par-Par, his speed is impressive.

Par-Par snorted as if it were obvious.

A dark blot appeared on the horizon, growing larger as they approached, taking on a familiar shape.

Tension left Li's shoulders. Quill.

Par-Par slowed to a stop. Quill whinnied and trotted up to them. Li slid from his mount and clipped a lead shank to her halter. He gave her a quick once over, looking for any obvious injuries. He didn't see any blood, and she appeared to be moving fine.

He hopped back on Par-Par, and they started their trek back.

Feeble rays of sunlight pierced through the clouds, attempting to brighten the soggy land. They did little to cut the wind's bite and soon disappeared as the sky threatened more rain. Li worried about Quill and her unborn foal catching a chill. He rode as quickly as he could, given he had to hold the lead rope in his hands—a downside to not having a saddle to tie it to. Thankfully, Quill was more than willing to cooperate, and they made it back without incident.

As they rode up, Li saw strange horses hitched outside the barn.

He halted his crew and dismounted. He frowned. Those weren't dwarven ponies. They were much taller, and their builds were sleeker, reminding him of Par-Par. *Horses from Sylandris?*

His gut twisted as uncharacteristic panic surged through him. Had he been found?

The barn door was open a smidge; he heard voices coming from it. Breathing slowly, Li focused on suppressing his aura, trying to hide its existence. Then, he quietly led his charges out of sight around the side wall, staying close enough to hear.

"The foals will be born within the next moon, likely sooner," said Taurin, a level of tension in his tone Li couldn't recall hearing before.

"Then we shall return near the summer solstice to see how things are progressing," said a new voice. "If they are not up to our standard, you know the consequences."

"They will be!" said Taurin, voice strained. "I've found an excellent stallion for the dappled mare."

Someone snorted. "We shall see."

Li heard footsteps as the visitors left the barn.

He carefully scooted around the corner so as not to be spotted as they mounted their horses and rode off. His heart nearly stopped when one of them paused, looking around the yard. Had they noticed his aura after all? After a tense moment, the rider signalled to their mount and left.

Based on what he'd overheard, the elves—the Elithar, he assumed by their weapons and amour—hadn't been there for him, and that was a relief. But what had they come for? Did Taurin owe them something?

He waited until the elves were long out of sight before he led Par-Par and Quill towards the pasture, wanting to make it seem like he'd just arrived.

"Taurin!" he called, releasing the hold on his aura.

Taurin poked his head out of the barn, looking white as a ghost. "You found her!" he cried, expression changing to delight as he hurried towards them.

Li handed Quill's lead rope to him. "And she appears to be sound."

They led the horses inside to give them a thorough grooming. Taurin conjured a stream of warm air to dry them off. "Do you think the foal is alright?" he asked, brow pinched.

"I believe so," replied Li, brushing Quill while Taurin dried Par-Par. "She wasn't gone too long. But we'll keep an eye on her."

Li touched Quill's huge belly. The red mare seemed perfectly fine, heartily eating out of the feed trough.

"Maybe I should send for Grimmst..." Taurin worried a lock of his hair, then put a blanket on her.

Li took his hand and gave it a gentle squeeze. "Let's see how she is tomorrow morning."

Rain began to fall as they made their way back up to the cottage. He debated asking Taurin about the imposing visitors but decided against it. Taurin would tell him if it was important.

It wasn't his business to pry, especially not when Li was hiding secrets of his own.

Chapter Nine

Hope

Taurin lay awake in bed, unable to sleep after the day's unwelcome excitement. Thankfully, Quill seemed fine, but he wondered if they should reach out to Grimmst anyway. Though he trusted Li that she was sound, he wasn't as versed in horse wellness as the old dwarf.

Then there were his unexpected visitors. The Elithar, the royal Sylandrian guard who protected the realm. He hadn't been expecting to see them until he'd sent for them, which wouldn't have been after the foals were born.

He shifted uncomfortably in bed, grateful Li hadn't been around when they'd shown up. From his looks alone, it was obvious Li was an outsider. Taurin feared the guard would have driven him away or taken him prisoner. Or worse. It wouldn't be unreasonable for them to think Li was a spy.

He replayed their conversation for what must have been the tenth time.

"You must have good offers for the foals by the summer solstice. Otherwise, you will be branded a criminal and banished from our lands," said the captain.

Taurin twisted and turned in bed, unable to bear the thought of not being able to return to everything he'd ever known. It was bad enough that his family had been forbidden from visiting him here on the plains. They'd stood up for him when he'd been on trial, suggesting that he raise horses for a suncycle instead of immediately being cast out of Sylandrian society. He would forever be grateful for their support and would not let this opportunity go to waste.

At least the ban is keeping Vardis away. Taurin didn't want to think about his previous partner, the one who had gotten him into this mess. Ugh.

Taurin had until the solstice to find buyers for the foals, but that felt like an impossible task. Though the mares would give birth soon, he doubted he would have any serious interest until they were a few moons old—after the solstice. He flopped an arm over his face. No one wanted to buy a foal soon after birth just in case they got sick or injured.

Giving up on sleep, he got out of bed and crept downstairs. He and Li managed to get the bed frame together, but Li insisted on sleeping on the couch until it had a mattress. Yet, Taurin couldn't help but wonder if there was another reason. He'd caught Li staring off into nothing a few times, and on the odd occasion the warrior wouldn't quite meet his gaze. *Have I offended him?* No, that couldn't be right. Li was just being shy about sleeping in the same space as him.

The tips of Taurin's ears prickled at the thought of Li watching him sleep. Li was so much nicer than Vardis. Taurin wished he'd noticed the signs before Vardis had betrayed him; how he always put himself first, whether it be during intimacy or out in public. He'd treated Taurin as a possession and discarded him when convenient.

Taurin hoped to never see his smug face again.

He tiptoed past Li's sleeping form, Nellie in her usual place on his broad chest. Once in the kitchen, he poured himself a cup of leftover tea from the floral pot. He magically warmed it and sat in a chair, idly plucking dead leaves from the small potted plant on the table. Perhaps it needed more sunlight. He gave it a boost of magic, watching its leaves soften before turning his gaze to the window. Outside, one of the silvery moons was nearly full. A moon that shone like Lily's coat.

Lily. What would her foal be like? As much as he hated to do so, he was betting everything on it. *Am I a fool?*

And if he were right about the foal's mystery sire, every noble across the land would be making him an offer. Perhaps even the illustrious king or the crown princess.

But Taurin didn't dare mention it until the foal was born, just in case he was wrong. He didn't want to get anyone's hopes up. *Not that anyone would believe me anyway.*

Li might, but—

"Are you alright?"

Taurin tore his gaze away from the window, meeting a topless Li with Nellie tucked under his arm. Instantly his face grew hot. He was glad Li couldn't see it in the moonlight.

By the moons, Li looked ethereal. Bathed in a beam of silver light streaming in from the window, it accentuated his muscles and sharpened his features. His long hair spilled over his shoulders like rich ink.

Taurin quickly looked away. "I was just thinking."

Li silently sat in the other chair and put Nellie in his lap.

Taurin fought with himself, debating whether he should tell his friend—lover—about the nature of the Elithar's visit. But he didn't want to worry Li, or worse, drive him away. What would he think if he knew the truth as to why Taurin was out here raising horses? That it was punishment for getting into trouble? No, it was best not to tell him anything about that until things were cleared up.

"I'm still worried about Quill and her foal," he said slowly, looking at his half-finished tea.

"They'll be fine. We made sure she was sound after her wet romp across the prairie."

"That isn't my only concern," he said, trying to build up courage.

Li patiently waited for him to continue, which Taurin appreciated.

"I'm also worried about Lily's foal. I don't know for sure who the sire is, but I have my suspicions."

"One of the dwarves' horses?"

He shook his head, golden locks swaying gently. "No, I think...I think it's one of the unicorns from the forest south of here," he said quietly, worried Li would laugh at him.

A pause.

"Is that so?" said Li. "How do you know?" He seemed to be taking this seriously.

Taurin let out a breath of relief. "During one of my first nights here, I had a strange dream. A unicorn from the Glimmering Forest had approached the pasture, making eye contact with me before leaping over the fence. He had passed through the wards without a ripple. I raced out there as soon as I awoke, but found nothing. The wards were undisturbed, and no strange auras lingered. I didn't find any hoof prints either. At first, I dismissed it as a stress-induced dream, but eventually Lily showed signs of being pregnant. I had Grimmst come to confirm."

"So, you think it wasn't a dream, but a vision," said the warrior. Gently putting Nellie on the floor, he got up and poured the last dregs of the teapot into a floral cup for himself. Steam wafted off it when he sat back down.

"It was too real not to be. I don't know how else Lily got pregnant," said Taurin, needing Li to believe him. "She's never been with either of my stallions."

"I suppose it's a possibility."

"What else could it have been? I would have known if one of the dwarves' animals got into the pasture, or anything else for that matter. My wards would have alerted me, but whatever it was concealed its presence. It had to be magical." Taurin spoke quickly, as if that would help persuade his companion.

Li set down his cup. "I can't think of anything else that would explain it. Do the unicorns typically leave the forest?"

He shook his head. "Never, and it's rare for those who venture into the woods to see them. They keep to themselves. We only go in to collect fallen strands of their hair, or, if we're really lucky, the horn of one who has passed on."

"What do you do with those things?" asked Li, dark eyes on him.

Taurin fidgeted. "We mainly make healing elixirs."

"Pardon my ignorance, we don't have unicorns back home as far as I know, but are they more intelligent than horses?"

"More so. They don't use language like us or the dragons. It is an entirely unique communication method known only to their kind."

A weight had lifted off his shoulders. Despite his apprehension, it felt good to tell Li. Taurin looked out the window again, the moonlight outside turning everything silver. The back of his neck prickled. Frowning, Taurin stood and focused his gaze towards the barn. His elven eyes allowed him to see in the dark, but he didn't see anything out there, nor did he sense any strange auras.

"Is something wrong?" asked Li, coming to stand beside him.

"I don't know. I think...I think I'm going to go check on the horses." A nagging in his gut told him to.

"At this time of the night?"

"Yes." He went to the door and pulled on his coat.

"I'll come with you," said Li, putting on his top.

"We don't both need to be up all night."

"It's fine," said the warrior, his tone suggesting there was no changing his mind.

Taurin was secretly glad for the company.

The storm had long since blown itself out. The moons were bright above them, bathing everything in their gentle light. Taurin all but ran to the barn, apprehension gnawing at him. Something was happening in there—he was sure of it.

He pulled open the door and snapped his fingers, soft orange light magically illuminating the lanterns. A few mares poked their heads over their stall doors, watching them curiously. Nothing seemed amiss. No animals had broken in, and there were no sounds of distress.

He and Li checked each stall just in case. As he neared the end of the row, he heard a low groan. Pulse spiking, he ran. Lily stood blinking at him in her stall, more or less perfectly fine. If not her, then who? He spun around. Han-Han lay on the straw, huffing and groaning.

The blood drained from his face. "Li!" It came out as a strained squeak.

Li materialized beside him. "She's in labour."

Taurin blinked "What?"

"Come on, let's get ready."

Taurin stood, rooted to the spot, wholly unprepared. It was too early, none of them were due for at least another half-moon! "But we need Grimmst!"

"We don't have time to send for him," said Li calmly. He gently grabbed Taurin's hand, snapping him out of his daze. "Get a clean bucket of water and some rags. If you have any elixirs to help with this, bring them too."

"I don't," said Taurin, wishing he'd had the foresight to get some from the dwarves. Brushing the thought aside, he found rags and a clean bucket, which he magically filled with warm water.

When he returned to the stall, they set to work.

"Hopefully the foal comes out the right way," said Li. "Otherwise it can get stuck, and that would be bad."

Taurin prayed that wouldn't be the case. Everything needed to go smoothly, for his sanity's sake, and for Han-Han. He couldn't bear the thought of losing her.

The dark bay mare flared her nostrils and groaned, covered in a foam of sweat. Taurin wanted to wipe it off, but Li held him back.

"We don't want to stress her out any further. I know you're just trying to help, but it's best to leave her for now."

Han-Han made another low noise.

Taurin instantly paled. She was starting to give birth, and it was messier than he expected.

Li knelt in the straw near her, bucket and rags at the ready. If the strange gooey sack coming out of her bothered him, he didn't show it. Taurin felt he might be sick.

"How long is this going to take?" Taurin asked quietly, moving to sit in the open stall doorway, willing as much fresh air into his lungs as they'd hold before slowly releasing it.

"Hopefully not too long. If all goes well, she should be done long before we see the sun's first rays."

He nodded, eyes glued to Han-Han.

She moved around as she tried to expel the foal from her body. Taurin feared she might accidentally crush it in her shuffling.

"It'll be okay," Li said softly.

Taurin desperately wanted to believe him.

The head of the foal appeared. "Good," Li murmured. "This should go well."

Time dragged on as Han-Han worked. With a great heave, half the foal slid out in a mess of fluid.

Almost there, thought Taurin. *You can do it.*

More grunting and pained fidgeting. The foal squirmed and kicked its front feet, uselessly trying to free itself.

Another effort from Han-Han had the rest of them sliding out. She went limp from exhaustion.

The foal struggled to escape the gooey sack.

"Should we help?" asked Taurin, eyeing the bucket.

"No, let her bond with him first," said Li. "She'll clean him up in a moment."

After catching her breath, Han-Han turned her head to her foal. She gave him a good sniff, then began to lick him clean.

"See?" Li carefully backed away, joining Taurin in the doorway.

Taurin found himself blinking back tears of relief. Tears of joy.

"Now to see if he'll stand. It's a good indicator of a healthy foal."

Quietly, they watched Han-Han clean her baby. The little colt had a dark coat, but with how messy it was, it was hard to tell if he was the same colour as his mother. And dark foals could lighten over time.

Eventually, Han-Han got to her feet. The colt, free of the revolting sack, struggled to do the same. Taurin hardly believed his spindly legs could hold him up, but the colt tried his best to gain independence. It took many tries, but eventually, he got all four legs beneath him and took a few wobbly steps around the stall before making a beeline for his mother. Soon, he was suckling happily.

Taurin's heart melted.

"He's a bit small, but he's a healthy one," said Li. "You shouldn't have any problem finding a buyer."

"No, I suppose not. Let's hope the other two are just as strong."

For the first time since leaving the forest, hope filled him. He was one step closer to returning home.

Chapter Ten

Lunch

Half a moon had passed since the birth of Han-Han's foal, and Li was still around. In that time, they had put together a straw mattress, so Li was no longer relegated to the couch. It was strange sleeping with Taurin so close by. He could hear the other elf shift around in his sleep. Part of him wished they had simply built one larger bed to share. Maybe it would have helped cool the fire inside him. Or maybe it would have fuelled the flames.

Taurin needed a lot of help with the foal. Though his knowledge of horse husbandry had grown, the foal made him anxious. He constantly asked Li for advice and second guessed himself. Li understood his concern; losing the little colt would be terrible. Taurin wanted to make sure the spindly baby grew up strong and healthy.

Thus, Li couldn't bring himself to leave just yet. Even if he tried, Taurin would likely have a meltdown. Perhaps he could go once all the foals were born, but what if the Elithar returned and kicked him out for being a foreigner? What if someone from the empire showed up? Sticking around was a huge risk, yet Li's desire to stay grew with each passing day.

He loved the horses; each had their own distinct personality that became very apparent once they grew comfortable around you. He enjoyed going for rides on the prairie, either alone or with Taurin, though they never rode east into the hills—his first few days there had left a sour taste in his mouth. He enjoyed speaking with the dwarves who stopped by to deliver food and goods while learning about their culture. And most of all, he loved being with Taurin. There was something about the other elf that had Li captivated. He frequently thought of their first kiss, their time in the barn. He was determined that the next time they did anything like that, it was someplace more comfortable.

It was a beautiful sunny day. The grass had turned from brown to gold, and the breeze was warm. Summer was coming. Li and Taurin were on their way to Greenwind, the nearest dwarven village, to have lunch with Matil; she'd invited them during her latest delivery to the stable. Li thought it was a good idea, since Taurin hadn't left the yard in days. He spent most of his spare time hovering around the pasture, watching over the colt, and waiting for the other mares to give birth.

"You need to step away," Li had said after Matil left. "Worrying isn't doing you any favours."

Taurin had been against it at first, but Li had eventually won him over. Still, Taurin fidgeted with his reins as they rode, causing King to snort and stomp until he stopped.

"The mares will be fine," Li assured him. "We cast those extra wards just in case."

"It's not predators I worry about."

Li gave him a look.

"Well, not just predators. What if they start to foal while we're gone? What if something goes wrong?"

"We'll be back by nightfall," Li patiently replied. "Horses typically go into labour at night."

"But not always."

"No, not always. We won't stay long. Matil knows we're expecting."

Taurin shot him an incredulous look.

Li flipped his hair over his shoulder, hiding his amusement. "Try to enjoy the day. We'll have our hands full once the other foals are on the ground."

Taurin rolled his shoulders. "I suppose you're right."

Before long, the village appeared in the distance, the buildings being the tallest things around on the flat prairie. Greenwind was made up of two rings. The inner ring held the bakery, the small smithy, and a few other shops, while the outer held homes made of stone with thatched roofs. A few other cottages were spread out on the prairie outside the rings. Matil and her partner Tagna lived in one of these homes just north of the village.

As they rode through, Li and Taurin quickly stopped by the bakery to pick up some wild berry scones.

Matil's home was a small two-bedroom cottage similar to the ones in Greenwind. Behind the house was a small paddock and a modest barn that housed two ponies and her wagon. A small vegetable garden off the one side was just starting to sprout. Colourful fowl squawked and pecked at the ground. They parted as the horses approached.

"Glad you made it," said Matil, opening the door at their knock—a door that was built for a dwarf, not a tall elf. "Don't you worry, it's warm enough that we'll be eating around back. I don't think either of you wants to spend the afternoon hunched over."

"We appreciate the consideration," said Taurin.

Li hadn't considered that they wouldn't fit inside until they'd visited the bakery, where he'd had to duck to avoid hitting his head on the ceiling's wooden beams. And the bakery was taller than the cottage.

"Tagna's just finishing the soup. Come, come," said Matil, leading them around back where a low table was set up. Instead of chairs, she'd laid out blankets and cushions on the ground for everyone to sit on.

"This looks lovely," said Taurin, handing her the box of scones.

Li nodded in agreement, settling himself on a cushion. "Do you need any help?"

"No, we've got it all handled," she said with a wink before disappearing inside.

Matil and Tagna brought out bread, cheese, and some sort of soup. Li wasn't entirely sure what was in it, but it smelled delicious.

"Lentils," said Tagna, ladling him a bowl. "They're easy to grow and you can dry them to store all winter. They're a great replacement for meat."

The soup was just as good as it smelled. The lentils had a certain earthy flavour, and the broth was packed with herbs and spices. Li had never had anything like it.

"Not all these spices are from around here, are they?" asked Taurin.

"Naw, some are from the south. A merchant came through last fall with a bunch of unusual things. Think this is the last of our stash."

"We're flattered you decided to share it with us," said Taurin, smiling as he ate his soup. He seemed to finally be relaxing.

"Pah, what's the point of having it if you're not going to share it?" huffed the dwarf.

"What's down south?" asked Li, dunking a slice of bread into the soup.

"Bit more grass, then a big ol' desert," said Tagna. "A hot, dry, sandy place is a good spot for spices. Dunno why. Sounds like a tough place to live. I can't imagine trying to keep your beard clean in a place like that."

Li had ridden through a desert before. While passing through the heat in armour had been very unpleasant, it hadn't compared to the sand that got into everything. He never wanted to experience anything like that again.

"So," said Matil, eyes twinkling. "Are you two official yet? When's your union ceremony?"

Both elves coughed into their soup.

"We're not—it's—" stammered Taurin, face red.

"With the mares foaling," said Li, coming to Taurin's rescue, "we haven't had time to consider something like that."

"Li's only been around for about a moon," mumbled Taurin.

"Mmm, that's fair," said Matil. She exchanged a look with Tagna, and Li's stomach tightened unpleasantly with guilt.

Their relationship would never reach that point. Not unless he knew for certain the Cloud Empire wasn't after him. And given how they treated elves like him, and the many resources at their disposal, that was highly unlikely. It was only a matter of time before they discovered he'd survived and showed up on Taurin's doorstep.

"Li?"

All three were looking at him.

"Ah—yes?"

"Are you done with your bowl?" asked Tagna.

He nodded. "Yes, thank you."

The dwarves cleared away their meal.

"You were right," said Taurin, smiling softly as the dwarves prepared tea and laid out the scones. "Coming here today was a great idea."

"I'm glad you're feeling better." He slipped his hand into Taurin's under the table and gave it a gentle squeeze.

Soon, the dwarves returned to the table with Taurin's scones and fresh tea, pouring it into clay mugs.

"It's our own blend," said Matil. "We foraged everything out here last summer." It was a sweet mix of herbs and flowers that was very different from the earthy tones Li was used to in the Empire.

"Do you sell it?" he asked after taking a sip. The mug was warm in his hands.

"Yup!" replied Tagna. "We take it to the market in town a few times a year. Takes a long time to collect all we need. You can't see it now, but we've been trying to grow many of these plants here." They pointed to what Li thought were flower beds encircling the cottage. "It's been slow going, but hopefully this year is a success."

Li didn't see how the flower beds would produce enough to sell, but perhaps they weren't trying to make a living off it. Matil did that with her delivery service. "I wish you all the luck."

"Luck, pah! Luck's got nothing to do with it. It's all about hard work and determination," said Tagna with an infectious smile. "I'll give you some leaves to take home."

"We'd appreciate that," said Li, the ends of his lips quirking up.

Once the tea and scones had disappeared, the elves said their goodbyes—after attempting and failing to help the dwarves clean up—and rode home.

"That's dwarven hospitality for you," said Taurin. "Guests aren't meant to lift a finger. We bought the scones, and that was more than enough. Some have given me a hard time for bringing along food to share." He chuckled.

"We'll have to invite them over to return the favour," said Li.

"Yes. Maybe after all the foals are born."

A tight knot formed in his stomach. Why had he suggested it? He wouldn't be around by then. It hurt seeing how Taurin's eyes sparkled with excitement, especially after how tense he'd been lately.

By the time they reached the barn, he was exhausted from trying to wrangle his emotions.

But the day wasn't over yet.

As he led the two stallions back to their pastures, Li noticed one of the mares lying on the ground.

"Taurin!" he cried, quickly loosing the stallions into their fields and all but leaping into the mares' pasture.

It was Breeze. She huffed and snorted, starting to stand, then laying back down. Her foal was on the way.

"Taurin!" Li called again, using his magic to amplify his voice.

The other mares stood nearby in a clump, tails swishing as they watched.

Taurin tore through the fence, wild-eyed and panting just as hard as Breeze. "Is she...?"

"Yes, I'll get supplies. You watch her."

"B-but, the barn?"

"We can't move her!" he exclaimed, already on the run. "We're doing this here. Now."

If Taurin replied, it was lost to him as he hurried to the barn for rags and warm water. When he returned, he could see the foal's hooves.

Taurin knelt on the ground near Breeze, looking very pale.

"It'll be fine," said Li, setting down the bucket and kneeling beside him. "Remember how smoothly Han-Han's went? She and her foal are doing well."

Taurin just nodded.

Li could almost see the bad scenarios running through his mind. "Hey," he gently grabbed Taurin's hand and squeezed it. "Deep breaths. We're here if something does go amiss."

It took Breeze longer than it did Han-Han, but much to their relief, a healthy filly eventually came into the world.

"She's the same chestnut colour as her mother," remarked Taurin as they wiped the mess off the foal. Breeze lay on her side, tired from her efforts.

"Once she's standing, we'll try to get them up to the barn," said Li.

Even with the wards, neither wanted to risk the new filly being left in the pasture overnight. Magic wouldn't protect her from the cool night air. She could easily catch a chill.

The sun had set by the time Breeze's foal was strong enough to make the walk. Breeze wasn't pleased about the move, pinning her ears back and showing her teeth to the curious mares that got too close. She even bit at Taurin as he led her, but he gently swatted away her attempts. She settled down once she and her foal were safe in a roomy stall.

"Two down, two to go," said Li as they approached the house. The moons were bright overhead.

"Hopefully Lily and Quill's births go just as smoothly..." Taurin picked at his nails.

"They'll be fine," Li assured him, putting a comforting hand on his slim shoulder. "What you're doing to keep your horses happy and healthy is working."

Taurin's small smile melted his heart. But the feeling was immediately snuffed out by a stab of guilt.

Chapter Eleven

Forest

Taurin wanted nothing more than to spend his days in the pasture, watching Lily and Quill. With the birth of Breeze's foal, his anxiety had increased while the length of his nails had decreased. Both births had gone seamlessly, which meant the other two could only go horribly wrong. That's how it worked, right? He needed them to go smoothly. And he needed Lily's foal to be part unicorn. If it wasn't...he didn't know what he would do. Hopefully, the sale of three foals—since one was already promised to a dwarven family—would cover his debt and prove to the court that he shouldn't be banished.

"Watching isn't going to make it come any faster," Li said over a cup of tea. They sat on some hay bales outside the barn, watching the horses while they took a break from their chores.

A few of the hens pecked at the ground near their feet while the orange cat stalked mice across the yard.

"I know," Taurin mumbled, fidgeting with his mug filled with the homemade blend the dwarves had given them. His journal lay beside him, untouched.

"We should go for a short ride, it's going to be a nice day," suggested Li.

There wasn't a cloud in the brilliant blue sky. Birds flew overhead, chirping, and insects buzzed about. The first wildflowers were starting to bloom on the hill, filling the air with their sweet fragrance.

But last time we went somewhere, Breeze went into labour. All of Taurin's being screamed that they shouldn't leave the yard. It must have shown on his face.

"We won't go far," said Li. "We can go south towards the Glimmering Forest."

The forest.

Taurin clenched the mug. "Maybe a ride is a good idea." The thought of being near the home of the unicorns helped to solidify his certainty that the sire was one of them.

They finished their break and chores, then saddled up their mounts.

No real trail led to the forest, as no one had any reason to go there; Taurin and Li forged their own through the growing grasses. None of the dwarves lived near the forest, though Taurin wasn't sure why.

"We just prefer the open skies," Matil had said when he'd asked. It was a bit of a strange answer, considering some of their people lived deep underground. But Taurin hadn't pressed the issue. Perhaps they simply didn't want to impose upon the unicorns' home.

And, if there was something dangerous in there that kept them away, Taurin was sure Matil or Grimmst would have told him about it.

The golden grasses rippled in the breeze, filling their ears with a gentle swishing that could lull one to sleep. Taurin took a deep breath, and the fresh prairie air and change of scenery started to settle his mind.

"Is it helping?" Li asked.

Taurin nodded. Anxiety still gnawed at him, but it no longer completely consumed him.

"Good. How far is the forest?"

"We can ride there and back by nightfall," he replied. "So long as we don't stop."

Li immediately picked up the pace. "Have you been to the forest before?"

"No, I haven't had a chance to explore it yet. I've only passed by at a distance."

"Then we want to get there quickly!"

Taurin appreciated Li's efforts to uplift his mood.

They loped and trotted along, the ground flying by beneath them. Before long, a dark smudge appeared on the horizon, growing closer at a steady rate.

"Aura's getting stronger," commented Li, slowing Sun, the golden mare.

"Yes." The aura emanating from the forest was difficult to grasp. From a distance, it was just a fuzzy jumble. But as they got closer, they could begin to pick out individual auras. However, what the auras belonged to was hard to say.

If not for his dream, Taurin would have no idea what the unicorns' auras felt like. He tilted his head, trying to sense them amidst the mass. After a moment, he gave up, unable to pick them out. Either the unicorns were skilled at hiding themselves, or their auras were weak. Taurin suspected it was the former.

They stopped when they reached the edge of the forest. Despite it being spring, the trees were fully leafed out. The wind rustled through the canopy, thunderous compared to the gentle swishing of the grass.

"We don't have to go in deep," said Li.

"I want to be back before nightfall, but we have a little bit of time to explore." Taurin urged King into the trees.

Bright sunlight filtered through the leaves, dappling the ground. Most of the forest floor was covered in thick undergrowth, but they were able to find some deer trails to follow. Or perhaps they were unicorn trails.

"Do you think we'll see one?" mused Li as they turned down one of the narrow tracks.

Taurin took the lead. "I doubt it. They'll sense our auras and stay hidden."

Li made a sound in his throat.

"Maybe if we're lucky, we'll find hair or something. It could be used to make simple healing elixirs."

"Do you know how to make them?"

"No, but there's an old dwarf who does, and some of the nobles back home do," explained Taurin, watching for any loose hairs snagged on the undergrowth. "Regardless, it would be good to have some on hand. A stray strand can still be useful on its own. See how the forest is already so green? It's because of the unicorns' influence."

Li picked something off a shrub as they rode past, then flicked it away. "Just spider silk. I wonder how their aura affects the other creatures that live here."

"I suspect they are all strong and healthy," replied Taurin.

Something suddenly chittered loudly overhead as if to agree. Both elves looked up, trying to catch a glimpse of whatever it was, but the creature was well hidden.

They rode in silence for a bit, taking in the wonders of the forest. The green foliage was interspersed with pops of bright colours where flowers bloomed.

Soon they came to a clearing. Sunlight shined brightly through the gap in the canopy, glinting off the colourful wings of butterflies that took flight when their horses stepped through.

"Tell me about your family back home," said Taurin, eager to know more about the elf stealing his heart.

"There isn't too much to say," Li began. "Both of my parents were warriors like I am. They served for their whole lives, just like their parents before them. They died while patrolling the northern border. My sword belonged to my mother. She was one of the strongest fighters we had."

"I'm sorry to hear that," Taurin said, heart clenching. "Do you have any siblings?"

"No."

"Me neither. It's uncommon for couples to have more than one thelim." Taurin held out a hand and a butterfly perched upon it. It was orange and red, like a brilliant sunrise.

"Some families have two or three offspring, but usually decades apart," explained Li.

"Is there anyone you miss back home?" He already suspected the answer, given that Li had no desire to return home, but he wanted to hear it from his companion.

There was a pause. Fearing he'd overstepped some boundary, Taurin turned in the saddle to look at him. The butterfly flew away. Li's expression was still relaxed, but he'd learned that the warrior was extremely skilled at hiding things.

"Not particularly," Li eventually said.

Taurin found that he believed him and mentally let out a sigh of relief. If Li didn't have anyone waiting for him back home, then he had no reason to leave.

"Aside from my parents, there's no one I particularly miss back home either," Taurin offered.

"Right, you said you weren't seeing anyone."

Taurin furrowed his brow at the thought of Vardis. "No, things ended between us right before I was s—before I came here. The relationship was very one-sided. Vardis only cared about himself. I was like an accessory to him. We would attend social events together, but otherwise, we only saw each other when he was in the mood for sex."

"He sounds awful," said Li, an uncharacteristically sharp edge to his tone. "I'm glad you ended it with him. Someone like that doesn't deserve you."

Taurin's ears prickled, Li's words filling him with warmth. He thought about telling Li what had truly ended their relationship, but he didn't know how Li would react. He feared the warrior would leave, and Taurin couldn't bear being alone again.

They soon reached the far edge of the clearing.

"Should we keep going or turn back?" asked Li.

Taurin peered up at the sky through the thick canopy. "We should probably head back soon. I want to be home before dark. But, if you don't mind, I'd like to sketch some of the flowers in the field. It's amazing how many there are so early in the season." He pulled his leather journal out of a saddle bag.

Li nodded. "Take your time. I'll look for some unicorn hair." He dismounted and tied Sun's reins to a low branch.

"Good luck on your search." Taurin stayed astride King while he drew. Was he sketching the flowers? Yes. Was he also sketching Li in the field of flowers? A small smile tugged at his lips.

They were about halfway home when Taurin suddenly pulled up his mount. "Li, stop," he said quietly. The warrior did.

Both their horses stood at alert, ears pricked to the west.

Beside him, Li narrowed his eyes, peering across the sea of golden grass. Taurin thought he caught a strange smell on the wind.

The ground before them suddenly erupted, clumps of dirt and grass flying upwards. The horses startled as a large, hairy rodent clawed its way out from below the ground.

"Just a *tahter*," said Taurin, making Par-Par turn circles to stop him from bolting.

The tahter was larger than the horses and covered in short, dusty brown fur with tiny eyes that were next to useless with large spade-like claws for digging through the earth.

"They're usually harmless," he said, his mount starting to settle. To his relief, Li had managed to calm Sun.

The tahter hardly paid them any attention, sniffing the air a few times before wandering off. It soon began to dig, disappearing from view almost as quickly as it had appeared.

"We don't have those back home," said Li. "But we do have giant serpents that live underground. They are very aggressive and territorial, with venomous fangs that can kill with a single bite. The older ones can swallow a horse whole."

Taurin shuddered at the notion. "Our serpents, called vernu, live in trees, looking like massive, feathered vines. They drop down and ensnare their prey, choking it out before consuming it. Some have magic they use to muddle the minds of their targets."

"I think we can agree that serpents are troublesome no matter where you are," mused Li.

"Yes," agreed Taurin. He loved learning about Li's homeland and vowed to ask him more about it. "As you can tell, tahters don't have aura, though I wish they did. That was quite a surprise. Fortunately, they tend to stay away from populated areas. Even our yard is too busy for them, despite them being underground. I don't think they like magic."

They reached home just as the sun sank below the tree line.

Li untacked the horses while Taurin raced to check on the mares.

"One, two—" Panic shot through Taurin like lightning. Quill lay in the middle of the field, surrounded by the other mares. She wasn't moving. "L-Li!" he choked out, throat closing up.

Blood roared in his ears as he raced over to her. He dropped to his knees in the dirt beside her. A metallic tang hung in the air.

"No, no, Quill." He looked for the rise and fall of her chest, but tears blurred his vision. He touched his hand to her side, praying, but felt nothing. The world swayed.

Strong hands steadied him. "Easy there," said a gentle voice. Li.

"Quill, she's—she can't be...her foal—" Taurin looked towards her tail. The ground lurched. She and her foal hadn't made it. He thought he was going to be sick.

"I'm sorry, Taurin," said Li gently, pulling him against his strong chest.

Taurin clung to him, gasping for air, Li's presence the only thing keeping him sane as loss and panic threatened to sweep him away. "What—I can't—all my fault."

Li gently rubbed his back. "No, it's not your fault."

"Y-Yes it is!" Taurin choked, tears streaming down his face. "If we hadn't left—if she hadn't gotten out in that s-storm—this wouldn't have happened!"

"Perhaps," was all the warrior said.

If only I hadn't been distracted with sketching!

The ride had been a mistake, one that had cost Quill and her foal their lives. And, a voice niggled at the back of his mind, made repaying his debt that much harder. He buried his face in Li's chest, breathing in the warrior's comforting scent as he cried.

As much as Taurin wanted to crawl into a hole and never come out, the world moved on. They couldn't leave Quill out here.

He took a few deep breaths, steeling himself, and rose to his feet. Li did the same.

"Thank you," he said quietly.

"For what?" asked Li.

"For being here. I don't know what I would do without you." He felt lost, but at least he wasn't alone.

Li, taking his hand, didn't reply.

An uneasy feeling twisted his stomach.

Chapter Twelve

Wyn-Wyn

There was a slight chill in the late spring air as Li strode over to the stable to muck out the stalls. Taurin had returned to the cottage to make breakfast after they'd checked on all the horses. Both were still shaken by Quill's death a few days ago.

Breeze watched him as he stepped inside her stall, her foal blinking curiously at him.

The two foals were doing well, growing stronger each day. Grimmst had come by right after Breeze's filly was born and declared that both she and Han-Han's colt were in good health.

"But keep an eye on 'em, an' give me a shout if anythin' happens," he'd said as he left. He'd given them a magical letter that could reach him instantly should the need arise. They'd sent him a non-magical message about Quill's passing.

Today, to help boost everyone's spirits, they planned on introducing Breeze's foal to the rest of the mares. When Han-Han had given birth, they had sectioned off part of the mares' larger pasture to give the new mother and foal their own space. Turning out a new foal with the rest of the herd wasn't safe, they could be seriously injured if the other mares decided to be unfriendly, so it was best to introduce them slowly and under strict supervision. The mares had been receptive to Han-Han's colt, so the pair now ran with the rest. But that didn't mean they would accept Breeze's. Horses worked in strange ways.

Li carefully cleaned around Breeze and her baby, not leaving a single patch of soiled bedding or pile of droppings behind. A clean barn was integral to everyone's health.

He gave the antsy mare a pat, knowing she was tired of being cooped up. "You'll be out soon enough," he told her.

She huffed again, clearly displeased with that. Li left her to it as he went to dispose of the muck.

After breakfast, Taurin haltered Breeze and led her to the pasture. Li followed behind, keeping an eye on her filly. They hadn't halter trained the foal yet, but they would start soon. For now, they trusted her to stick to her mother, which she did.

Taurin made an opening in the fence and let Breeze loose. The mare instantly took off, hopping and bucking around the field. Her foal awkwardly followed her, staying by the fence while her mother burned off her pent-up energy. Li smiled as he watched Breeze.

The mare suddenly came to a stop and looked around.

"Seems like she forgot about her foal," said Taurin with a trace of amusement, the most he'd shown over the past few days. With a flick of his wrist, he smoothed out the top of the hedge so they could sit.

Li climbed up beside him. "If I had to be cooped up for days, I'd be restless too."

"You were," said Taurin, poking him in the side. "After I found you, I could barely keep you on the couch—you were on the barn's roof the next morning."

Li looked away. "Lies."

"Pfft." Taurin's eyes glinted—a good sign. He'd been lifeless the past few days, methodically going about their chores without speaking, and often staring into the void. Li tried to take on more of the load to make it easier on Taurin, but Taurin said work was a good distraction.

They turned their attention back to the mother and daughter. Now that Breeze had calmed down, her filly had returned to her side. But when she got close to the fence separating them from the rest of the mares, who were slowly gathering to check out the newcomer, her baby stopped.

"She's shy," remarked Taurin.

"She's never seen so many horses before."

"But Han-Han's colt went right up to them." Taurin fidgeted with a strand of hair.

"You know that doesn't mean anything." He put a reassuring hand on Taurin's shoulder. "They all have personalities just as unique as ours. Give her time."

Taurin grunted. "I guess."

Breeze approached the mares, sniffing them. Most she hardly reacted to, but one or two had her pinning her ears back and baring her teeth.

"They're not going to hurt your baby," Li called to her.

She ignored him, but her ears flicked back up. After a few minutes, she returned to her foal who wouldn't move past the middle of the small pasture.

The other mares stayed close to the fence but returned to their grazing. Han-Han and her colt kept their distance. The little guy stayed with his mother, but he was interested in the newcomer on the other side.

"They're all relaxed," Li said.

"Except our new filly."

The gangly foal stood beside her grazing mother, head up and ears pricked towards the rest of the herd.

"She'll figure it out, especially since her dam is so calm."

Li's words rang true. After a few moments, the foal relaxed and turned her attention back to her mother to nurse.

They watched the pair a while longer.

"Who do you think we should bring into their pen first?" mused Taurin, breaking a bout of peaceful silence.

"Normally, you would want to introduce the horse with the highest rank in the herd first. In this case, Sparrow is the leader of the mares."

"Yes, she was good with Han-Han's colt."

"Right. But, your filly seems shy, so maybe someone with a gentler nature to start," Li suggested.

"Lily?"

Li shook his head. "No, she's too close to foaling. She might try to take the filly as her own."

"That happens?" Taurin asked incredulously.

"Yes. Haven't you seen her try with Han-Han's foal?"

"I thought that was Han-Han being temperamental..."

"Nope. But Lily will stop once she has her own." Li stretched, starting to get sore from sitting. Even though Taurin had magically smoothed it out, the top of the woven fence wasn't the most comfortable. "I was thinking Sun," he nodded towards the palomino near the back.

"Mmm, I was really hoping to have her bred," said Taurin, watching the golden mare graze. "But I couldn't find a sire."

"She has excellent conformation, and a fairly smooth gait." He'd enjoyed the few rides he'd taken her on.

"And a gentle disposition. You're right, she would be good to introduce to little Wyn-Wyn—tomorrow."

They both agreed that Wyn-Wyn needed more time to get used to them—and to being outdoors in general. Once she was comfortable in the pen, they would bring in Sun.

It took nearly half the day before Wyn-Wyn was at ease outside. Eventually she left her mother's side and started exploring, even going up to the curious mares on the other side of the fence. Watching her bound around, stretching her long legs, was a delight.

"There you go," said Li the next day. He tried to shoo the mares away from the dividing fence while Taurin herded Sun through an opening he'd created. "See how confident she looks? Everything will be fine."

Wyn-Wyn watched the chaos with dark, curious eyes. But instead of being nervously glued to her mother's side, she proudly stood a few steps away, ears perked, tiny tail swishing.

Once Sun was in the pen, Taurin closed the gap. He and Li took up posts on the fence, carefully monitoring the three. Sun ambled over to the pair, ears forward. Breeze watched her but showed no signs of stress or aggression.

The two mares touched noses, taking in each other's scent. Wyn-Wyn moved behind her dam, unsure of the golden newcomer.

Breeze suddenly pinned her ears back and bared her large teeth, but Sun hardly reacted. Instead, she calmly walked a few paces away and started grazing. She showed no interest in Wyn-Wyn.

"Did she not see her?" asked Taurin, nervously picking at one of his nails.

"Sun definitely knows Wyn-Wyn is there." It was impossible for her to miss the foal who was now cautiously stepping towards her, tiny nostrils flared as she took in the larger horse's scent.

Sun turned an ear towards her but didn't lift her head until Wyn-Wyn was right beside her.

Wyn-Wyn bared her front teeth and repeatedly clacked them together—something all foals did when meeting older horses to show they were harmless babies.

Sun gave her a good sniff but was otherwise uninterested.

Breeze stood behind her baby, keeping a close eye on both of them.

Li relaxed as he watched the horses. While things could still turn sour, it was becoming less and less likely. Taurin still looked tense. Li put a reassuring hand over his. Neither spoke, not wanting to disrupt the peace.

Wyn-Wyn, confidence growing, nosed Sun curiously. Sun shook her neck as Wyn-Wyn nibbled at her mane. When the filly didn't stop, she jerked her head up, startling Wyn-Wyn who swiftly retreated to the safety of her mother's side.

Taurin let out a low breath.

"They're fine," said Li, squeezing his hand. "Wyn-Wyn needs to learn her manners. And Sun taught her so very gently. See how Breeze isn't bothered?" The mare in question stood calm while Wyn-Wyn began to nurse from her. "If she thought her foal was in danger, she would have gone after Sun."

"I suppose. Should we bring another in?"

"No, we don't want to push it. We should end this on a good note. Let's give them another day or two."

"Alright," Taurin agreed, squeezing Li's hand in return.

A soft smile tugged at Li's lips, followed by a painful pang. Leaving this place was going to tear him apart...

They left the three horses together for a while longer, taking turns watching them while doing chores. Wyn-Wyn, once she'd recovered from her spook, investigated Sun. Sun let her, occasionally correcting the baby.

"Has Sun had a foal before?" Li asked when they returned her to the main pasture.

"Yes, I was told she was bred twice before I got her," said Taurin, "and successfully foaled both times. Some of the lower nobles bought the foals. Why?"

"Her behaviour around both our foals suggests she's had one before. Unlike Sparrow," he nodded towards the bay mare, "who is cranky around the little colt."

Even now, Sparrow had her ears pinned back as the colt accidentally ventured too close. He immediately bounded away.

"She's always cranky," commented Taurin, sealing up the hole once Sun was back with the main herd. "Do you think she will settle when she has one of her own?"

Li haltered Breeze. "Maybe, but she might also get worse. Ah—not towards her own foal," he quickly added, seeing alarm flash across Taurin's face. "While it does happen, it's rare for a mare to reject her foal outright."

Worry still pulled at Taurin's face as they led the pair into the barn. "Do you think Lily will reject her foal?"

Li wasn't entirely convinced the sire was a unicorn; either stallion could have gotten into the pasture in the night. As for the lack of evidence, Taurin might have overlooked something. He's seen the golden elf do it before when he was particularly anxious: spilled tea, a dropped pitchfork. "I can't say for sure, but it's very unlikely."

"I would like to conduct a small ceremony for those who didn't make it off the boat," said Li that evening. He'd been mulling it over for a while. It didn't sit right with him that, as the sole survivor, he hadn't honoured their passing. Given how and why they'd left the empire, he doubted anyone there would. "We can include Quill and her foal in it too, if you want."

Taurin blinked, pausing in his cooking. "Absolutely!" he said, recovering. "When do you want to do it, and what do we need?"

Despite the gravity of the request, a small smile tugged at his lips. Taurin's willingness to help filled his heart. "I don't need much. Just some candles and an open space."

"We've got candles and lots of space." Taurin's brown eyes flicked to the window.

"I'd like to do it at sunset this evening, if possible."

"Of course! There should be some spare candles upstairs. Please, help yourself."

"Thank you." Li went to fetch the candles.

The sun set with a fiery rainbow of colour. Reds, oranges, yellows, that all slowly faded to dark blue—fitting for those who had burned with such passion and bravery. Leaving one's homeland wasn't a choice made lightly, especially when you'd spent your entire life serving it. Li only wished others would start to see the empire the way he had. That things were not as good as they appeared to be. That blindly following orders wasn't always the right thing to do.

He knelt on the ground in a quiet part of the yard, facing the sun. His heart twisted at the sight of the circle of candles burning before him: one for every fallen warrior and the two horses. Too many. Too many lives had been lost that day. Tears pricked at the corners of his eyes.

Taurin knelt beside him, expression sombre. His presence was a great comfort.

They watched the sun's final rays fade away. As the last of the light disappeared, Li snuffed out the candles with a gentle gust of air. His heart ached as he watched the smoke spiral upwards, eventually disappearing.

"The flames represent their lives," he quietly explained after a moment of silence, throat tight. "The smoke carries their spirits to whatever lies beyond. This ceremony is done at sunset to signify the end of a cycle."

A gentle hand touched his shoulder.

"I wish I could have done something for them, but I..." his words died in his throat as grief consumed him. He took shaking breaths as tears flowed. Li knew there was nothing he could have done against the power of the storm and the sea...but maybe he hadn't tried hard enough. Maybe he if he'd just...

Taurin's hand moved from his shoulder to his back, gently rubbing it.

"I'm sure you did all you could," Taurin said softly. "And I bet they appreciate that you've done this to honour their memory." He wrapped his arm around Li, letting his own tears fall.

"Thank you," Li whispered, leaning into the much-needed touch. Taurin's words didn't ease the overwhelming sense of loss, but he appreciated them all the same.

They stayed like that for a while, only moving once Taurin started to fidget, not used to kneeling for so long.

"Alright, we can go back to the house," said Li.

They collected the candles and headed up the hill to the cottage. Despite the nature of the ceremony, a weight he hadn't known he'd been carrying was lifted off Li's chest. Taurin was right: he'd done everything he could. And the best way to honor their memory was to live a fulfilling life.

When they reached the cottage door, he pulled Taurin into a hug.

"Hey! We're dirty!" Taurin protested. In the light of the cottage, their leggings were covered in dirt and grass from kneeling.

"Not as dirty as we could be." He smirked as Taurin's face turned bright red. "Removing clothes will remove the—"

Taurin silenced him with a quick kiss. "Fine, but let's do this inside."

Li all but dragged him through the door. They hardly reached the sitting room before their lips crashed together, hot and needy.

Taurin pressed against his firm body, groaning as Li's strong hands squeezed his soft ass. "Li..." he breathed into the kiss, eyes lidded.

Li slid one of his muscled hands around front, touching Taurin's growing need. The golden elf shuddered, knees going weak. It was a nice change from the gloomy mood that had settled over the cottage.

He stepped forward, guiding Taurin down onto the worn couch.

"What are you doing?" Taurin asked, tips of his ears red.

"Let me take care of you," Li said, sinking to his knees between Taurin's legs and staring up at him with his dark eyes.

Taurin swallowed. "A-Are you sure? You're the one who needs—"

"Pleasuring you will help," said the warrior, tone husky. He needed a distraction from his sorrow, to feel like he wasn't alone in the world. "Besides, I think you need it too."

"Alright..." said Taurin, voice airy.

Li quickly got to work, freeing him from the confines of his leggings. Taurin bit his lip as Li gently gripped him, their eyes locked together as he opened his mouth and lowered his head.

Taurin inhaled sharply as Li's tongue touched his member.

Slowly, Li ran it up and down along him, savouring his flavour.

Taurin groaned, eyes lidded, legs tense on either side of him.

By the empire, Taurin looked *divine*, like a gentle golden god descended from the heavens. The sight filled Li with a burning heat, piercing through the heavy sense of loss that had settled over him.

He took the tip of Taurin's hardened member into his mouth.

"Gods..." Taurin breathed, eyes squeezing shut.

Li groaned around Taurin as a hand tangled in his hair, sending flashes of heat straight to his groin. Fuck. Spurred by his own mounting desire, Li took him deeper, throat and tongue working together. Had Vardis ever pleasured Taurin like this? Given what little he knew of Taurin's previous partner, Li doubted it. Vardis was a taker, not a giver.

The hand in his hair tightened its grip as Taurin pressed back into the worn leather couch, breathing heavily. "Li-Liander," he breathed, voice filled with need. It was clearly taking all his restraint to keep his hips still.

Ignoring the urge to gag, Li took him all in, determined to worship him like the god he was.

Face flushed, Taurin's free hand flew to his mouth, and he bit down on a knuckle. Had anyone else ever seen Taurin like this before? Li secretly hoped he was the only one to have earned the privilege. It was a sight for only the worthiest of devotees.

"L-Li, I'm—!" Taurin barely got out before he tossed his head back with a loud moan.

Li greedily swallowed like someone who'd stumbled upon an oasis in the desert.

Taurin went limp on the couch, strength fleeing him.

"You're beautiful," Li whispered, resting his head on Taurin's thigh.

Taurin opened a bleary eye. "I'm not," he mumbled.

Smiling, Li slid up his body until they were face to face. Their lips met gently this time, yet there was no denying the desire still burning in their eyes—a desire both wanted nothing more than to spend the night indulging.

But Taurin suddenly pulled away. "Did you hear that?"

Li tilted his head. "No?"

Taurin frowned. "It sounded like—"

A faint squealing echoed across the yard.

Lily.

They both leapt up from the couch, the mood evaporating.

"We'll finish this later," said Taurin, hastily fixing his leggings before rushing out the door. The apologetic look on his face did little to quench the fire still burning within Li.

"I'll be right out," he hollered after Taurin, voice strained.

Damn it.

Chapter Thirteen

Moon

Breeze and Han-Han shifted nervously in their stalls while Lily grunted and groaned in hers. She was lying down, snorting and panting. Taurin rushed in, heart beating like he'd just run the entire breadth of the Manwan Plains. He would not lose another foal. *He couldn't.*

"Easy there," said Li, patting his shoulder. "Horses pick up our energy. You need to relax or you'll stress her out even more."

Taurin nodded, throat dry. This was the moment he'd been waiting for. The foal had to be fine, it had to be healthy. And, most importantly, it had to be part unicorn.

Li went to prepare a bucket of hot water and some rags, but Taurin couldn't bring himself to leave the stall. His heart still beat like a drum and his hands were clammy. This was it. Soon he'd know if he was going home—or if he'd be banished. His vision blurred; Taurin took a few deep breaths to center himself. Now wasn't the time to lose his nerve to anxiety.

Lily rose to her feet, trying to ease her discomfort.

Taurin wanted to go to her, to pet her neck and soothe her, but he stayed where he was. To his relief, Li soon returned.

"How is she?"

"Alright, I think." His voice was hardly more than a squeak.

"Everything will be fine." Li took his hand and gave it a squeeze.

Taurin nodded, desperately wanting to believe him.

"The others went well, and based on Grimmst's last check, Lily is in good health," Li continued.

But what if the foal isn't? So many things could go wrong. And even if the birth went well, there was the possibility that he had been nothing but a fool all these moons and the foal was simply an ordinary horse.

Lily lay back down, grunting and huffing as her body strained. She squealed loudly again, sides heaving. Tiny hooves appeared.

Something flicked across Li's face.

Taurin's pulse spiked. "Wh-what's wrong?" he asked, muscles seizing up as panic grasped at him.

"I think the foal is backwards," said the warrior, dropping his hand and moving into the stall.

Taurin's insides went cold. He stood there, frozen. A foal that came out rear legs first could easily get stuck, threatening their life and that of their dam. *No.* Not again.

He tried to say something, but his voice wouldn't work properly. "—mst."

"What?" said Li, trying to get Lily to her feet.

"We need Grimmst," he choked out.

Li shook his head. "He won't arrive in time. The foal could die if we don't do something right now."

His urgency helped ground Taurin, who stepped into the stall. "R-Right."

"We need to get her up," Li said, "If the foal's legs are positioned correctly we might be able to save them both."

Taurin nodded, taking deep breaths. He joined Li in trying to get the grey mare to her feet.

With their gentle but persistent urging, she rose.

"Good, now we can help pull the foal out."

Taurin blinked, thinking he'd misheard. The sight of Li pulling off his top, exposing his muscled chest and arms, only confused him even more.

"What are you...?"

"I'll help pull it out. It's going to be messy. You keep her standing."

"Have you done this before?"

Li stepped right up behind Lily. "No. But we have to try."

Taurin nodded stiffly. He stood at Lily's head, cooing and gently petting her neck as she groaned, trying to expel her foal. He wanted to cast a calming spell on her but worried it would interfere with the birthing process.

No, I'm the one who needs the spell. With each passing moment, his anxiety grew; his heart felt like would explode out of his chest.

He glanced back at Li, covered in mess and pulling on something. Taurin was about to ask how it was going when a spark flickered in the warrior's eyes. A thrum of magic washed over them. Lily made a deep rumbling sound in her chest.

"What was that?" asked Taurin, his voice high.

"Trying to get it unstuck," Li said, face twisted in concentration. He was just as sweaty as Lily. "Didn't work. I don't want to pull too much harder and risk damaging the foal's legs. But we need to get it out now—it could suffocate."

Not knowing what else to do, Taurin put a hand on Lily's side. He closed his eyes and reached out with his magic, feeling for any sign of an aura. He'd tried to detect something from the unborn foal before to prove that it was part unicorn, but he'd never been able to sense any magic—the same as a normal horse. But maybe now it was time...

A bright aura flicked in his mind's eye: Li. And another further away: the wards he had on the pasture fence. He ignored both and continued to search.

Come on.

It wasn't easy, and he began to lose hope. But when Lily shifted her weight, he felt something. The tiniest wisp of aura. He immediately latched onto it, careful not to overpower it with his own.

Knowing one wrong move could put the foal at risk, he magically applied force, matching Lily's efforts, trying to help push the baby out.

They worked in silence, Lily's strained huffing and snorting filling the barn.

"Almost there," said Li. "Once the hips are out, things should get easier."

It felt like he'd been casting for an eternity. This was taking too long—even Lily had stopped pushing to take a break. How could the foal possibly be alive after all this?

Taurin's concentration slipped when Lily tried to lie down. "No, you need to stay up," Taurin said, knowing Li could only help the foal while she was standing. He quickly resumed his spell.

But the aura suddenly disappeared.

"There!" said Li. There was a wet sound as the foal slipped out. Lily let out a huge sigh.

Taurin dropped the spell and hurried over to where a very messy Li was gently setting the foal down.

The exhausted mare turned and lay down, beginning to lick her foal clean.

"Is it alive?" breathed Taurin, throat tight, terrified of the answer.

"Yes. She's alive." Li's tone wasn't reassuring.

"But?"

"Coming backwards was hard on both of them." Li stood. "I'll send a message to Grimmst." He strode outside. There was a burst of aura as he sent the magical missive.

Taurin stared at the foal. Compared to the other two, she was tiny. She lay on her side, unmoving save for the rise and fall of her chest.

Taurin grabbed some rags and magically warmed them. He carefully rubbed her down, not getting in Lily's way as she bonded with her baby.

Li returned and put a hand on Taurin's shoulder. He hadn't realized he was shaking until then. Fear and anxiety filled him, making his stomach churn. The other foals had tried to stand not long after their births, but this one wouldn't even raise her head. A head that was devoid of any horns.

Taurin's heart clenched, but he reminded himself that most animals weren't born with horns; they grew with age. And maybe a half-unicorn would never grow one. If not for the aura he'd sensed, he would have thought her a normal horse. Yet it was nearly impossible to detect when he tried to feel her aura now. He thought he was going to be sick.

"We need to get her to nurse while we wait for Grimmst," said Li, cutting into his downward spiral. "Since she can't stand, we'll have to bring the milk to her."

Taurin nodded and flew out of the stall, the task helping to keep his anxiety at bay. He found a pail and a bottle and quickly returned with them.

"Hey, Lily," he said, approaching the exhausted mare. Lily barely paid him any attention. Thankfully, she seemed to be fine after the ordeal. He was worried his magic could have harmed her. "I know you're sleepy, but I need you to stand up again for me. We need milk for your little filly."

"Have you ever milked a horse before?"

"No, have you?"

"Not horses specifically. Sit with the foal. I'll do it."

Taurin handed him the pail and got cozy in the straw. He carefully pulled the foal's head onto his lap, petting her thin neck. Her coat lightened in colour as she dried. She was darker than her mother, but many greys were known to be nearly black at birth.

He reached for a fresh towel and warmed it, glad they had brought so many into the stall. He continued to wipe her down. The last thing she needed was to catch a chill.

Li managed to get Lily to her feet and, after a few moments, in which Lily seemed very displeased, came with a bottle of milk. He held it to the foal's lips, but she made no effort to drink. "This might be tricky..."

"Try squeezing some in?" suggested Taurin, pausing his rubbing.

"She might choke." Instead, Li dripped some onto his finger and stuck it in her mouth. "If we can get her to taste it, she might clue in." He rubbed the inside of her lips.

The tiny foal grunted, but otherwise didn't react.

Li kept at it, wetting his finger over and over and rubbing milk against her teeth.

Taurin's hopes soared when she feebly licked her teeth and were instantly dashed when she did nothing more.

Lily gently nosed her baby, but the foal hardly responded. She rumbled unhappily, worried.

"We're trying to help her," said Li, petting the mare's dappled grey neck. "We'll get her up."

"At least Lily's not rejecting her," said Taurin—a small relief.

"No, she's not. One good sign. Sometimes, they'll reject a weak foal, knowing it won't survive. But Lily is interested in this little one."

Taurin nodded and warmed the towel again, continuing to rub her down. She was drying off quickly under his ministrations. "I want to name her Moon."

"Just Moon?" asked Li. "Not Moon-Moon?"

Taurin shot him a displeased look.

A red spark suddenly flashed before them. "That means Grimmst has received the message," said Li, staring at the spot where it had faded. "He'll be heading over as quickly as he can."

The news did little to ease Taurin's nerves; it would be a while before he arrived, even if he rode the fastest pony the dwarves had. "Should we lift her and see if she gets her feet under her?" Maybe that would spark some fight in her.

Li thought about it for a moment. "We can try, but honestly, I don't think it will help."

"I want to try anyway." He needed to do more than sit here with her. Waiting was killing him.

"Then if you hold her front, I'll handle her rear." Li moved the pail and bottle out of the way in case the foal suddenly kicked. Either of them could lift her by themselves, but it was better to be safe than sorry.

Taurin slid his hands under Moon. Together they gently lifted her.

Come on. Taurin willed her to move. To react. Hope sparked in him when she moved her head, stopping it from flopping, but she didn't flail or kick as a healthy foal would. She didn't even try to get her legs under her, letting them dangle loosely.

Taurin was still determined. They lifted her until her tiny hooves no longer touched the straw. Taurin held his breath as they gently lowered her as if he were afraid it would knock her over. Would she attempt to hold her weight?

They tried to steady her as she made contact with the ground, Li using one hand to position her legs into a sturdy stance. But to their disappointment her legs immediately buckled. They gently lay her on the straw. She blinked feebly at them.

Taurin let out his breath, imagining all the swirling emotions within him leaving with it. It didn't help. His future was riding on her survival.

And if they couldn't get her up, he would never see Lyrellis again.

Chapter Fourteen

Grimmst

Taurin stayed with Moon and Lily all night. Li came and went, bringing in supplies like fresh towels, and checking on the horses and chickens once the sun crested the horizon. Nellie had taken up a post on a spare towel in the aisle of the barn, clucking every time he passed by. He didn't want to leave Taurin, but life still went on regardless of the state of the little foal.

At one point, he found Taurin crying over her and feared the worst. He hurried into the stall but saw her side still slowly rising and falling. She hadn't left them yet.

He stood beside Taurin and put an arm on his shoulder. "Come with me for a moment. We're crowding Lily." Taurin didn't want to leave, but Li coaxed him into the aisle. Taurin wrapped his arms around him, burying his head in his shoulder as Li gently stroked his back, giving him time.

Eventually, Taurin lifted his head. "She can't die. I need her to survive..." His eyes were puffy, his face stained with tears.

"We all want her to live," Li said softly.

"I know..."

Li waited for the but. One he suspected had to do with the Elithar's visit after the storm.

Taurin took a few deep breaths and let go of him.

Li dropped his arms, waiting.

Taurin fidgeted with a lock of his golden hair. "I need her to live because I owe a debt of sorts."

A debt? He raised an eyebrow. "So, you owe coin to someone?" Starting up a breeding stable wasn't the fastest way to earn gold—if it even managed to get off the ground.

Taurin wouldn't meet his eye. "Sort of."

Sort of? He waited. Pushing Taurin would only worsen his anxiety.

"Something happened back home. I did something I shouldn't have, and got caught."

Li blinked. Taurin, this gentle, anxious elf doing something illicit? He couldn't believe it.

"Because I come from a reputable family, instead of casting me out, I was offered the chance to redeem myself by turning this forgotten stable into a successful breeding venture. And that I had a little over a suncycle to do it. If I'm successful, I can return home. And if not, I'll be banished from Sylandris forever."

Li blinked, stunned. Banished? What? Why? Whatever could Taurin have done that was worth that kind of punishment? And he only had little over a suncycle to do it? That wasn't a very long time, given that horses had a gestation period of nearly a complete cycle.

"And no one is allowed to help?" Li asked stiffly.

"No one wants to be associated with a criminal, even a temporary one," Taurin explained. "When I return home, it will be a while before the other nobles stop shunning me."

If it were up to him, Li wasn't sure if he would want to return to a place like that. Situations like this were one of the reasons why he'd left his own homeland. "What did you do?"

Taurin fidgeted, not meeting his eyes. A tense moment passed before he spoke. "Vardis and I were messing around with some magic, and things went awry. No one died, but some homes and trees were damaged as a result. He fled, leaving me to shoulder the blame once the Elithar showed up."

Li crossed his arms, annoyance flaring. "And he never owned up?"

"No. Not before I left."

"Slippery coward!" Li hissed vehemently, making Taurin jump. How dare he do this to Taurin? To this kind, sweet elf? He'd disliked the greedy noble from the moment Taurin had first spoken about him, but this—this was beyond low. If Li ever ran into Vardis, he would make him *pay*.

"This is all because I tried to stop him," Taurin continued nervously, as if he expected Li to turn on him at any moment. "But he wouldn't listen. I thought what he was doing wouldn't work, so I tried to stop the magic, and it blew up instead." He let out a shaky sigh. "And now I'm here."

Li didn't speak, too angry with the situation. Perhaps it was best that Taurin was here; it meant he was away from that asshole.

"I was given a small amount of gold to start things up. Which I also have to pay back. So I need all the foals to survive and sell for good prices to pay off the damages, the loan, and prove that I'm worthy of Sylandrian society."

So this was why Taurin hadn't hired anyone, nor could afford to pay him a wage—not that Li minded. He stayed because he wanted to.

Li wanted nothing more than to race to Lyrellis and beat Vardis to a pulp. Instead, he closed the gap between them, wrapping his arms around the quivering elf.

"Moon would solve my gold problem," said Taurin, leaning into him, "and prove to everyone that I meant no harm. Unicorns don't appear to those with ill intent, and they certainly wouldn't breed with their horses. You believe me, right?" The desperation in his eyes pulled at Li's heart. By the empire, how would he ever be able to leave this elf?

"Of course I believe you." He gently kissed Taurin's forehead. "We will make sure Moon survives. For her sake and yours."

Grimmst arrived just after sun-up.

"Sorry I'm late," he said, hopping off his pony. "Was out north of town."

"Don't worry about it," said Li, hitching the pony while the older dwarf untied some bags from his saddle. "We're just glad you're here. I can grab you some breakfast while you check out the foal."

"Tha'd be appreciated." He set off towards the barn.

Li hurried to the cottage and grabbed him some food before joining them. When he arrived, Grimmst was greeting Lily, making sure she was comfortable with his presence around her foal.

Li stayed out of the stall, not wanting to crowd her. He handed Grimmst the promised breakfast.

"Hmm, she not standin'?" said the dwarf, biting into the bread. He patted Lily with his free hand. The mare slowly relaxed.

"No, she won't even try..." Taurin answered, still cradling the foal's head in his lap.

"Not good," said the dwarf.

Taurin went pale.

"And ye said the birth was rough?" Since Lily was relaxed, he squatted down to take a look at Moon.

They gave him a rundown of everything that had happened.

"Yer very lucky," said Grimmst. "It could'a gone a lot worse." He carefully checked the colour of Moon's lips, which Li could see were pale even from where he stood.

"She's got no energy. We gotta get some milk into her." Grimmst ran his hands along her body, pressing and prodding at different places. "Feels cold."

Taurin immediately grabbed and warmed another towel from the pile Li had brought from the house during the night, ready to cover her once Grimmst was done.

"Not sure if that'll help. Not in the long run." The old dwarf closed his eyes and held a hand over her.

Li sensed aura stirring in the air around him. Interesting. He knew Grimmst was one of the few dwarves who could use magic, but he'd never actually seen him use it before. It was different from elven magic. It was…rougher? No, just less fluid. If elven magic was as free-flowing as the wind, dwarven magic was sturdy like a rock—which he supposed made sense because Grimmst could only use magic related to the earth. Elves could wield all sorts of magic, but dwarves were limited to one or two elements each.

Grimmst's magic was soothing. He was doing his utmost to keep Moon comfortable. "She has an aura?" he said, furrowing his bushy brow, magic fading. "That can't be…"

Li met Taurin's eyes and gave him an encouraging nod.

"I think…" mumbled Taurin. "I think her sire is a unicorn."

Grimmst blinked at him before dropping his gaze to the tiny foal. "If that's the case, there's nothin' I can do. My magic won't be strong enough."

Taurin was on the verge of tears. Li wanted to rush over to him, but the dwarf suddenly continued.

"Ye might want to find her sire. I don't know much about unicorn foals, but there are stories about both parents bein' around at their births."

If Grimmst said there was nothing he could do to save the foal, then as much as he wanted to argue, Li believed him. But finding the foal's sire? That was a lot to ask. He'd be a few hours' ride away in the forest and tracking him would be nearly impossible. Their previous ride there had shown him that. Only Taurin could find him—that is, if he remembered what the unicorn's aura felt like. A unicorn he'd supposedly encountered in a dream.

And Taurin was in no shape to do that now.

Li looked at Moon. By the sun, she was so tiny. They were running out of time. He picked at the wooden stall door, not knowing what to do. Should he race off to try to find the stallion, or stay here and see if they could devise another solution? He wasn't confident about either idea. It was a shame he'd never learned more healing magic beyond tending to simple injuries, but they had healers for that in the empire. He'd been trained in the art of combat instead.

"You really think the stallion can help?" Li asked slowly.

Both Taurin and Grimmst looked at him.

"I don't know," Grimmst answered. "Like I said, it's what's in our stories about them horned critters."

Li met Taurin's sad eyes. His heart clenched at the sight of the heartbroken elf cradling the tiny foal. Mind made up, he let go of the door and went to saddle Par-Par. Hopefully, this wasn't a mistake.

As he tacked up Par-Par, footsteps approached. To his surprise, he turned to see Taurin, another saddle in his arms.

"I'm coming with you," said the golden elf, determination blazing in his eyes. "Grimmst said he will watch over Moon."

"We owe him big time," said Li.

They caught and saddled King, then rode off into the night. Despite the dire situation, Li couldn't help but admire how the moonlight glimmered on Taurin's hair. He vowed to do whatever they needed to once they reached the unicorns' forest; Li never wanted to see that heart-wrenching expression on Taurin's face again. Yet he knew he would.

Li leaving the farm for good would break both of them.

Chapter Fifteen

Search

They rode swiftly, the ground disappearing beneath their stallions' hooves—though not fast enough for Taurin's liking. *Go, go, go!* he urged King, wishing they could move faster. He and Li hardly said a word as they flew across the prairie, too focused on guiding their mounts. The grass, while not yet at its full summer height, hid many dips and holes that could easily break a horse's leg.

Taurin spent the whole ride praying that Moon would be alright. That she would pull through this. He hated leaving her alone with Grimmst, but he didn't think Li could find the unicorn stallion on his own. Besides, the determination in the warrior's eyes had lit a fire in his belly. He couldn't sit around and wait while Li—kind, caring, beautiful Li who owed him nothing—raced to save Moon's life. Moon was his responsibility.

After an eternity, a dark smudge appeared on the horizon.

"Nearly there," muttered the warrior beside him.

Taurin's heart leapt. *Finally*. He closed his eyes, feeling the auras whorling around in the trees, but they were still too far away for him to pick anything out.

"Sense him?" asked Li.

Taurin opened his eyes and shook his head. "No, but I'm not very skilled at tracking auras."

"I'm sure you'll pick up the stallion's trail once we're there."

He appreciated Li's confidence.

They halted their mounts once they reached the edge of the woods. The thick forest didn't look very inviting in the dark, but that didn't dissuade them. They dismounted and led their horses on foot, giving the stallions a much-needed break. They couldn't exhaust them now, not when they still had to ride all the way back.

"You did so well," said Taurin, patting King's neck. They wove their way around through the trees, occasionally stopping for Taurin—and sometimes Li—to try to detect the stallion's aura.

"Still nothing," said Taurin, shoulders slumping.

"It's a large forest. They'll be around here somewhere," Li assured him.

"But what if they're not? What if they've left?" Worry gnawed at his stomach, making him feel queasy. So much was riding on this.

"Why would they leave?"

"I don't know..."

"They're still here. They're just hiding," said Li matter-of-factly.

They swung up onto their mounts again, urging them into a slow trot as the trees opened into a clearing.

"This is where we turned around last time," observed Li.

"Then we continue on," Taurin said, something in his gut telling him they were going the right way. Last time because he'd been worried about his horses, but now he wondered if there had been more to it. Something magical.

They crossed the clearing and stepped back into the trees. King snorted just as a fuzzy feeling washed over Taurin's head.

"A ward," said Li, tilting his head. "I've never felt one like that before."

Taurin reached out for the stallion's aura, and a dizzying explosion of whorling colours filled his mind's eye. He immediately pulled back into himself, overwhelmed. "There's so many..."

"Wards?"

"No, auras," Taurin said, "It must be the unicorns. They've let us through."

The trees on this side of the ward seemed livelier than those on the other side. Perhaps it was the way they swayed in the breeze, or how their tops seemed to reach for the sky; they were greener and lusher.

"The unicorns' influence." Li nodded at a bush already covered in bright red berries when most outside the ward were still flowering.

Closing his eyes and mentally preparing himself, Taurin sought out the stallion's aura again. It was hard to pinpoint anything in the gale of aura battering his magical senses. Slowly, he worked to pick them apart. The ward was the easiest to detect because of how powerful it was, but it muted everything else. Taurin did his best to ignore it and focus on what was hiding underneath, but he was having very little luck. It was frustrating.

A hand suddenly enveloped his, startling him.

"Keep at it," said Li, not meeting his eyes. "I'll help."

A steady stream of aura flowed into him from his companion. It was calm and gentle—a dark blue. But there was a strange undertone to it, one that prickled the edge of his already heightened anxiety. If not for the dire situation, Taurin would have asked what was bothering the warrior.

Li's aura pushed at the ward's energy, keeping it away. Immediately the other auras became more noticeable. Taurin picked through them, taking his time even though he wanted to rush. Hurrying would get them nowhere.

Some of the auras belonged to plants, or to creatures who remained hidden amongst the trees, their cries occasionally filling the air. But the brightest ones had to belong to the unicorns.

"I feel them," said Li softly. His hand remained in Taurin's as Taurin opened his eyes and guided them along an invisible path.

They rode so close to maintain the connection that their boots occasionally bumped together.

Eventually, they slowed to a stop in a spot that looked no different from what they'd been riding through. "We're here," said Taurin, letting go of Li's hand. He looked around and frowned. He could sense the unicorns, clear as day, yet couldn't see them anywhere. He fidgeted with his reins.

Li turned Par-Par in a circle. "They're here. I think they're testing us."

"Probably." Taurin prayed it was so. He couldn't bear the thought of coming all this way—and leaving poor little Moon—just for nothing. "We mean you no harm," he said, projecting his voice and aura into the trees. "We've come seeking your help."

"Can they understand us?" the warrior quietly asked.

"Maybe not our language, but supposedly our auras."

Yet there was no response from the trees—no stamping of hooves, snorting, nor any shifting of aura that would indicate a response.

Li started looking himself over. "See if any of her fur is stuck to you."

Taurin checked himself, pulling a few dark hairs off his sleeve, short and soft enough to belong to a tiny filly. Holding them out, he addressed the forest again, "Your foal has been born, but she's unwell. We've tried everything we know to help her, but she won't eat. She doesn't even have enough strength to stand. Please, help us save her!"

The wind gently rustled through the trees. Taurin hardly dared breathe. Had they heard him? Was the fur enough, or should they have brought Moon with them? No, they could never have safely transported her so far.

"Please..." Tears pricked his eyes. "She's going to die without your help." He dismounted and lay the hairs on the ground, unsure what else to do.

There was a soft thump. A hand gently touched his shoulder. Li stood beside him.

"They have to come," Taurin breathed, afraid that speaking might scare the unseen unicorns away.

"Let's give them some space," said Li, nodding at the hairs on the ground.

They led their mounts away and waited. Taurin was really starting to despise waiting. He played with a strand of King's mane, wanting to tear out his own hair. It took everything he had to keep still and quiet.

The auras suddenly shifted. Taurin held his breath. They both intently watched the spot where he'd placed the hairs.

Perhaps he was imagining it, but Taurin thought he heard soft hoof beats over the gentle wind in the trees.

The sound grew louder, the auras stronger.

If he had blinked, he would have missed a unicorn stepping into existence before them.

The stallion's snow-white coat gleamed in the darkness as if it were made of moonbeams. He had a long horn that looked to have been spun from the clearest glass. His mane cascaded gracefully down his neck, his tail a flowing banner behind him.

Long hair grew on his lower legs, covering massive hooves. He was larger and stockier than the stallions the elves had ridden in on.

There was no mistaking the aura emanating from him: it matched the one Taurin had felt in his dream all those moons ago.

The stallion sniffed the hairs, taking in their scent. Neither elf said a word as he lowered his horn. The hairs lit up, reflecting off the crystalline horn and throwing shimmers of refracted light across the clearing. The stallion's horn began to glow in response, the shimmers disappearing. He raised his head, his piercing liquid gaze causing Taurin's breath to catch.

The unicorn walked slowly forward, horn lowered. Taurin's instincts told him to move out of the way of the deadly point, but he stood his ground. He had no reason to be afraid. He was the one who had sought the stallion out. The tip touched the right side of his chest where his damis resided.

Colours filled his mind's eye as emotions crashed over him. He felt joy, loss, fear, sorrow. It was overwhelming, and he wanted to fight back; it took every ounce of willpower to keep still and let it happen. Every now and then, he caught a glimpse of his own memories. He was experiencing the unicorn's life, and the stallion was observing his.

After an eternity, the stallion removed his horn. It all vanished, leaving Taurin feeling drained. His knees buckled, but strong arms steadied him.

"Thank you," he mumbled to Li.

"You're welcome."

The warrior let go sooner than he would have liked. That strange uneasiness returned, giving Taurin the sense that he'd done something wrong. He straightened up, strength returning, and blinked in confusion. "He's gone."

The stallion and the unseen herd had disappeared. Only their auras could be felt, but they had grown faint.

"They've moved deeper into the forest," said Li, peering into the distance, not seeing anything through the undergrowth. "Did the stallion give you any answers?"

"Yes." He strode over to where Moon's hair had been. A pointed clear stone matching the stallion's horn sat in their place. Had he snapped off the tip? Taurin picked it up, marvelling at how it caught the faint moonlight filtering through the leaves, giving off an iridescent sheen. It radiated with the stallion's energy.

"We need to take this to Moon."

He passed it to Li, who quickly examined it. "Amazing. I've never felt anything like it. I thought it might be similar to kirin magic, but it's very different."

Taurin didn't know what a kirin was, but he didn't ask as he took the shard back and put it safely in a small pouch hanging off his belt.

They both swung up into their saddles and turned their horses back towards home—towards the little filly whose life was hanging on by a thread.

Hopefully, they weren't too late.

Chapter Sixteen

Euphoria

They made it back in record time. Li's heart lifted at the familiar view of the yard. Strange...he hadn't been around all that long, but he already considered the stone cottage home. Leaving would tear him apart. But now wasn't the time to worry about that.

He and Taurin hurried into the barn, midmorning sunlight flooding in behind them.

"We're back," panted Taurin.

"Ah, good," said Grimmst.

"How's she doing?" asked Li as Taurin entered the stall, the clear shard already in hand. Lily lay on the bedding, her foal curled up beside her.

"No changes."

While that wasn't the best news, it was far from the worst. No one had expected Moon to improve while they were away.

"You find the stallion?" asked the old dwarf.

"Yes, he left us this," Taurin held out the shard.

Grimmst touched it with a wrinkled finger. "Mm lots 'o magic in that. What do ye do with it?"

"We're not sure," said Li, leaning on the stall door. Grimmst stepped into the aisle, gesturing for him to join Taurin. He gratefully did.

Taurin knelt down beside Moon and held it out to her nose. The tiny foal blinked, then lifted her head to sniff it.

"That's the most interest she's shown anything," remarked Li, squatting beside him. It had to be a good sign.

Her velvety nose brushed against the shard. It flashed and a wave of aura rolled over them. The stallion's aura radiated strength and power, but there was also a sense of calm and comfort. He cared about his foal.

Moon snorted like dust had gotten up her nose, the first real noise she'd made. The stallion's aura wrapped around the filly like a blanket. She snorted again, ears perking up.

"It's working," Taurin breathed. Guided by something he could only assume was the stallion's aura, he gently pressed it to Moon's head, right where a horn would grow. The magic around them grew stronger and the iridescent shard glowed with a faint light.

Taurin furrowed his brow.

"What's wrong?" asked Li.

"It broke in half."

"What?" Sure enough, the crystalline point had split in two straight down the centre.

Moon moved her head. One of the bits touched above her eye.

Taurin sucked in a breath. "Oh no, it's stuck to her." He let go of it. The shard stayed in place, off-centre on her forehead.

"Try putting the remaining point above her other eye," said Li quickly, sensing Taurin's rising panic.

Taurin did. It, too, stuck fast.

"Hmm, I'd say they're her horns now," said Grimmst, watching from the open door. "My, I never dreamed of seein' anythin' like this! Fascinatin'!"

Moon shook her head, as if dislodging a bothersome fly, looking livelier by the moment. The shards softened into small nubs, the sort of horns you would expect to see on a young animal. The shards' light dimmed, and the stallion's aura faded.

Moon gathered her legs under her.

"Is she...?" said Taurin.

Li nodded, watching as the spindly foal tried to stand.

Lily slowly rose beside her, showing her how it was done.

Both elves moved towards the door, giving them space to move.

Taurin wanted to stay close by in case she fell, but Li held his hand. "She needs to do this on her own."

The golden elf nodded, never taking his eyes off Moon. "The two horns are a little strange."

"It'll be fine," replied Li.

It took a few tries before Moon could get her legs to cooperate. Li held Taurin back when she fell head-first into the bedding. A few attempts later, with falls that seemed to cause Taurin more distress than anyone else, Moon got all her legs beneath her and stood. She looked so proud and strong. Even without the bumps, there was no doubt in anyone's mind that there was something special about her.

She was wobbly on her feet, but that didn't deter her from taking a few shaky steps towards her mother. Taurin's hand tightened around Li's.

Lily made an encouraging sound as Moon nosed at her belly, eventually finding her milk. Soon she was eagerly suckling away.

Taurin's grip on his hand relaxed. "She did it."

"You did it," said Grimmst, eyes shining. "You saved that little one."

Li hardly noticed. Riding high on their success, he turned Taurin towards him and planted a kiss on his lips. Taurin eagerly returned it, tears of happiness streaming down his face.

"I'll be off now, boys," said Grimmst, pulling them back to the present. "Now that yer filly's up, try to get some rest." There was a knowing look in his eye.

The mood in the stall had shifted. Gone was all the tension and heartbreak, replaced by relief and euphoria.

And something else.

They bade farewell to Grimmst, remaining in the stall to watch Moon a bit longer. But Li was feeling antsy. The kiss had reignited his unfulfilled needs from last evening. He put a hand on Taurin's shoulder, wishing his needs would flow to his companion.

Just as he was considering taking a walk to cool his head, Taurin spoke. "Grimmst is right. We should head to bed."

Li's heart leapt. A spark in Taurin's eye had him all but dragging Taurin up the hill to the cottage.

Once they reached the door, they flung off their boots and hurried up the stairs, laughing as they nearly got stuck in the narrow passage.

Clothes were hastily discarded. They fell onto Taurin's bed, lips crashing together.

Heat flooded through Li, pooling in his groin. With one hand planted beside Taurin's head, Li straddled the golden elf, careful not to break their kiss, as his inky hair formed a dark, intimate barrier around them. His other hand ran up and down along the outside of Taurin's soft thigh.

Taurin sighed into the kiss, immediately pouting when Li broke it off.

"We need that vial," Li said, voice husky.

"Top drawer," Taurin replied quickly, his eagerness evident in more ways than one.

Li hastily fished it out of the carved wooden nightstand beside them. He poured a generous amount on his hand, but instead of slicking up his growing need, he stroked Taurin's.

Taurin squeezed his eyes shut, body going taught. The sight alone sent heat straight to Li's groin, driving him mad, but he didn't stop.

"Li..." Taurin breathed, face flushed.

Li stopped and pressed one of his slicked fingers to Taurin's heat. Spreading Taurin's legs and kneeling between them, he gently worked it in, admiring how the soft muscles on Taurin's stomach tensed. A light sheen of sweat coated them.

"Beautiful," he murmured, dipping his head down to nip at one of the pink buds on Taurin's chest.

Taurin's toes curled, legs flexing with pleasure.

"Keep still for me, would you?" It sounded like a request, but his tone suggested otherwise.

Taurin nodded, trembling legs ceasing their movements. It was taking a lot for him to obey.

Li's finger pressed and prodded, loosening and slicking Taurin's hole. It was soon joined by another, then another. Taurin mewled softly with each addition, the sound only fueling the fires of Li's desire, wearing down his patience faster than ice in the blazing sun.

He kissed a trail down Taurin's chest, the taste of salt tingling his tongue. He straightened up and removed his hand, pouring more of the slippery fluid onto it. Li let out a low growl as he slicked up his own hard member.

Taurin watched him through one lidded eye, following the movement of his hand.

"Patience." It came out as little more than a hiss. Once it was thoroughly coated, he pressed it to Taurin's tight heat.

They both groaned as it slid in. A lesser elf might have released on the spot, but Li had been raised a warrior. He had pride.

Planting his hands on either side of Taurin's shoulders, he began to move.

Arms wrapped around him, the touch hot on his skin. Taurin blinked at him with hooded eyes, face flushed. Their lips met again, gently this time, savouring each other. Taurin tasted sweet, like crushed pine needles, with a tangy aftertaste of spiced tea.

Li's movements quickened, unable to get enough of the intoxicating elf beneath him. He couldn't remember the last time being with a partner had been so enjoyable. From the sounds Taurin was making and the way his nails dug into Li's back, the sting mixing with pleasure, he felt the same way.

He stroked Taurin's manhood, hand moving in time with his hips. Taurin broke their kiss, letting out a low moan that could just be heard over the sound of slapping flesh.

Li's lips went for the soft skin of Taurin's neck, nipping and kissing. Taurin's tightness squeezed him, nails raking down his sides.

"Fuck," Li growled, pleasure-pain rippling through him.

"I'm g-going to—Li—"

"Hang on a bit longer." His hand was wet from Taurin's member. "Together." He buried himself in the tight heat, seeking release. They were so close.

Taurin moaned with each hilting thrust, back arching as he rubbed against Li's hand. "Li, I can't..."

"Almost—" Wrapping his free arm under Taurin, he pulled him close. Taurin nipped at his neck, the sudden pain shooting straight to his groin. He returned the gesture, teeth leaving a mark that would most certainly still be there in the morning.

Taurin tightened deliciously around him in response. With one final deep thrust, they both cried out, seeing stars as their climax crashed over them.

Li collapsed on top of Taurin, panting. The arms around him loosened as strength fled Taurin's body, but he didn't let go. Li buried his face in the crook of his neck, inhaling his sweaty, post-euphoric scent.

"I love you," said Taurin, voice little more than a hoarse whisper.

Li didn't reply, the words a sudden knife to his heart. Why had he done this, knowing he had to leave?

Taurin didn't seem to notice his silence, already starting to doze off. Li freed himself from his embrace and lay beside him, stomach churning.

He had to leave—and the sooner, the better. Not just to protect Taurin from the Empire, but to protect his own heart.

What am I doing?

Chapter Seventeen

Breakfast

Taurin was alone in bed when he woke the next morning. This wasn't surprising since Li was usually the first one up. Yet something slithered unpleasantly in his gut. Li hadn't returned his declaration of love last night, and he'd felt the warrior pull away as he'd drifted off to sleep. What did it mean? Perhaps nothing. Li could have been just as exhausted by the day's events as he was; the warrior was good at hiding things. Maybe he was being a bit paranoid after having such a disastrous relationship with Vardis.

Taurin went downstairs and was greeted by the sound of the front door closing. Taurin looked out the kitchen window, seeing the dark haired warrior making his way down the slope to the pasture, Nellie following close behind. Li had his sword on him, meaning he must be planning to run through some forms like he often did once he was done his chores. Nothing odd about that.

He prepared and covered a pot of tea for them to have with breakfast later, then set out to join his partner. It was cloudy out, but there was no scent of rain on the wind.

He met Li in Par-Par's pasture. He was petting Oak, the red gelding who kept Par-Par company. "Good morning," Taurin said brightly.

Li grunted a response.

Taurin's brow furrowed. He stepped closer to look at Li's face. "Are you feeling sick?" He prayed that were the case.

"I'm fine," said Li curtly, turning his head away.

"Okay," Taurin said, a strange tension filling the air. "I'll go turn out the mares."

Li, running his hand down Oak's leg to check for injuries, merely nodded in response.

Taurin went to the stable, unable to shake the tightening knot in his stomach. Had he done something wrong? Li had never acted like this before. Sure, there were a few times when Li wouldn't meet his eyes, or had broken off a touch too soon, but they wouldn't have had an intimate night if something were amiss between them, right? Yet worry gnawed at his insides as he led the pairs of mares and foals into the pasture. It didn't start to abate until he returned to check on Lily and Moon. The tiny foal was curled up on the floor, but lifted her head at his approach. She stood up and stepped closer to her mother, wary of him.

Taurin couldn't help but smile. "I'm glad you're doing well, little one. Hopefully we'll have you two outside before long."

Moon flicked an ear. Lily came over and nosed him, looking for treats. He fed her a carrot from his pocket. "You did so well," he said, rubbing her forehead as she munched.

He refilled her hay net, checked her water, then returned outside. Breeze and Wyn-Wyn were still separated from the rest of the herd for now, but he and Li had expanded their paddock to give them more room to run. He put Han-Han and her colt in with them. Seeing the foals playing and bouncing around filled him with hope. He was going to get through this, once word of a half-unicorn got back to Sylandris, he knew all the nobles would be clamouring to purchase Moon. His heart tightened at the thought of selling her, but he'd known from the beginning he couldn't keep any of the foals.

He checked on the rest of the mares, eventually joined by Li—sort of. Li still wouldn't look at him and didn't speak a word.

The strange mood between them returned.

"I brewed a pot of tea before I came out," said Taurin, magically weaving branches back together behind them as they exited the pasture. He tried to keep his tone light, hoping it would help with whatever was going on with Li.

"I'm going to muck out the stalls first," came an emotionless reply.

"Oh," said Taurin, deflating like someone had magically sucked all air out of him. "Are you sure?" They always had breakfast together.

"I'm not hungry." Li abruptly turned off towards the barn, leaving Taurin alone.

He must be feeling unwell, Taurin told himself as he collected eggs from the chicken coop and returned to the cottage with Nellie to prepare breakfast. But Li looked perfectly healthy, and there was nothing in the way he went about his chores that suggested otherwise.

His palms broke out in a cold sweat. What had he done to upset Li? Was the sex that bad? It certainly hadn't seemed like it last night. Li had even been the one to initiate...

Taurin lit the stove and cracked the eggs into a pan with some butter, still lost in thought. Hmm, had Li perhaps received some news from the empire? Taurin wasn't sure that was possible; they had no idea where he was, and he'd never seen Li trying to contact them. He would have noticed if Li had reached out to them by any magical means.

He tipped the fried eggs onto two plates, adding slices of bread topped with cheese. Though Li said he wasn't hungry, it didn't feel right not to prepare some for him. Taurin sat at the small table, watching the barn out the window, occasionally feeding Nellie bits from his plate. The hen clucked as she plucked them from his hand.

Li eventually emerged, but he didn't come up to the cottage. Instead, he drew his sword and started practicing different cuts. Right, he'd seen Li take his sword out with him.

Taurin quickly finished his meal, then picked up the plate he'd prepared for Li. "Come on, Nellie." She followed him down to the yard, then went off to visit the other hens.

"I've brought you breakfast," he said, carefully setting the plate on top of a large bucket beside him for Li to grab once he was done.

"Thanks." Li's tone was still devoid of emotion.

"Has something happened?" Taurin asked gently, afraid of being shut out.

"No."

Tense silence filled the air.

Taurin picked at his nails, trying to build up the courage to ask what was wrong. If he'd done something, he wanted to know so he could fix it.

"Do you have buyers?" Li suddenly asked, swinging his sword with expert precision.

Taurin blinked, caught off guard. "Um, for one of them, sort of."

"Sort of?" A downward cut punctuated his words.

"To pay for the wood and paint used on the barn."

"Right, you mentioned that before. What about the others?"

Li had been such a huge help the past while, of course he was concerned about their efforts paying off. And about Taurin repaying his debt. "I haven't looked for buyers for them yet."

"Shouldn't you have been working on that from the start?" There was a strange harshness in his tone.

"I—I," he fumbled, mouth going dry at Li's sudden shift. It wasn't helping that the warrior still wouldn't look at him, focusing entirely on his movements. Taurin's tongue didn't want to work properly. "It's likely one of the dwarves will take the other horse, but I'm hoping someone from back home will buy—"

"Likely? Hoping?" He stopped mid-swing. Li finally looked at him, face stony.

It took everything Taurin had not to look away.

"What are you doing here, Taurin? You should have had buyers lined up long ago."

"But I didn't know if the foals would make it." His voice kept catching in his throat. Why was Li acting like this? What had he done to upset him?

"That doesn't matter. You should have been reaching out to prospective buyers. I hope those snotty elves who came by when Lily ran away are interested in purchasing."

Taurin's blood went cold. "The Elithar aren't interested—"

"Right, of course not," Li snapped. "Who are you hoping will buy Moon? The royal family themselves? That's a lot to stake on one foal who we didn't know would even survive until now. What would you have done if she hadn't made it? If she hadn't been a unicorn?" He sheathed his sword and stepped towards Taurin, face twisted in anger.

Taurin stepped back, knocking into the bucket—and the plate of eggs, which went flying everywhere when it hit the ground. He tore his gaze away from the mess, chest tightening. "Li, I—"

"Save it, I don't want to hear it," Li cut in harshly.

"But—"

"I'm leaving."

The ground dropped out from under him. "What?" This couldn't be happening. Li's anger made no sense. *Maybe I should have looked into buyers for the other horses sooner, but not for Moon.* He hadn't confirmed her ancestry until yesterday! This couldn't be what Li was so angry about. "Li, wait!" He stepped toward the warrior, but Li turned away. "Li, please, talk to me! Whatever I've done, I can fix it!"

Li didn't answer, nor did he look back as he strode off into the prairie.

"Li, come back! Don't—don't abandon me like Vardis did!" Taurin stood rooted in place, too shocked to follow him. He rubbed his eyes, hand coming away wet.

But the warrior kept going, the long grasses soon swallowing him up.

Taurin sank to his knees. A choked sob escaped him as his heart shattered to pieces.

Taurin moved about as if in a hazy dream. He had little memory of completing the day's chores, body moving on its own. The horses and Nellie seemed to notice that something was wrong, both by Li's absence, and Taurin's misery. He did little besides caring for the animals, wandering listlessly around the yard. Nellie followed him wherever he went, clucking quietly.

A sudden squealing later that afternoon jolted him from murky depths. Both stallions were on high alert, watching the western sky. They bucked and reared, trumpeting a challenge.

The geldings snorted and pawed at the ground. Taurin raced out of the barn where he'd just been sitting with Lily on Moon. Following their gaze, he scanned the clear sky. He saw nothing save for the dark speck of a bird high above.

But the speck was quickly growing larger, and a strange rumble followed it. A smoky smell filled the air, agitating all the horses.

Taurin's stomach dropped like a ball of lead. That was no bird. "No," he whispered, eyes wide.

The magenta dragon let out a deafening roar as they swooped low over the pasture. The mares took fright, running and bucking.

What should I do? His magical fence kept out most threats, but even with the extra wards Li had added, he knew it wouldn't be enough to stop a dragon. They were just too powerful. And until now, he'd never seen one this far east.

The dragon pulled up, then circled around for another pass.

The mares thundered across the field, the foals in the smaller pen barely keeping up with their mothers. Taurin magically dropped the inner fences between them all. The males instantly raced to the mares, their tails streaming out behind them like war banners. But how could the herd take on a dragon?

What are you doing here, Taurin? Li's hurtful words echoed in his mind. The warrior was right, what was he doing? He was just a noble who had no idea how to raise horses. He'd relied on Li for so much, but now the warrior was gone. Driven off by his own incompetence. What Taurin wouldn't give to have him here now, he would surely know what to do against a dragon.

Shaking, Taurin raced into the field. "Hey, over here!" he cried, waving his arms as he sprinted. Drawing the dragon's attention was foolish, but he had to do something.

Ignoring him, the dragon swooped again, jaws open. There was a bright spark in their throat.

"No!" he screamed, uselessly throwing out his hand as fire burst forth.

Chapter Eighteen

Blaze

Don't abandon me like Vardis did!

Fuck. Taurin's words were a knife to the heart, and Liander hated himself for it. But he'd done what he needed to protect Taurin and the horses. If he hadn't acted now, he never would have left, the Cloud Empire would eventually find them and raze everything to the ground. They would show Taurin no mercy for harbouring a deserter.

Besides that, their intimate night had felt so *right*—and that scared him.

His heart ached and his legs were heavy as he walked further and further away, leaving everything behind. What he'd said to Taurin had been unforgivable, but he needed to drive a wedge between them. At least if Taurin hated him, he wouldn't be compelled to follow.

Yet he wanted nothing more than to turn back. Each step was harder than the last, but he'd lived the life of a warrior; he'd made tough decisions before, like choosing which dying comrade to save, or ending the life of someone who couldn't be helped. This was no different. Despite trusting his logic, his heart was breaking apart, the pieces scattered in the tall grass behind him.

It wasn't long before the rippling golden sea obscured everything from view.

In hardly more than the blink of an eye, every familiar part of this land was gone. He regretted not grabbing the map, but his departure had been more sudden than anticipated. When Taurin had approached him with breakfast, he knew he had to do it then, or he would have lost the will.

Now, he travelled into unknown lands with nothing but his sword at his side. At least this time, he wasn't exhausted from being shipwrecked, and the weather was much warmer. He debated looking for one of the dwarves' paths, but didn't want to be spotted travelling along them. Word might get back to Taurin, or worse, to the empire.

Taurin would have a bad time when the indigo-clad warriors showed up. Li should have warned him, should have told him why they were after him. But hopefully, Taurin would just point them on their way, and they would leave with no fuss. Really, they had no reason to interrogate him more than that. They didn't know Li had been living there for over a moon and had no reason to suspect it unless Taurin brought it up. He didn't believe the golden elf was foolish enough to do that. Like the

Elithar, Taurin would want them out of his hair as quickly as possible.

Still, should he have told Taurin? If things got bad and they tried to search Taurin's mind—he prayed they wouldn't—they would discover that he didn't know Li was on the run. That he hadn't known he was harbouring a fugitive. And that would work in his favour.

Li's pace slowed, steps hesitant. But the Cloud Empire might not care; that Taurin had looked after Li at all would be enough for them to condemn him. They'd killed over far less—which was one of the many reasons why Li and the other warriors on the boat had left.

No, Taurin would be fine. He was letting his desire to return cloud his judgment. Besides, the chance of them even finding the stable was slim. They were more likely to run into the dwarves…who would point them to the stable. He clenched a fist. *Damn it.*

Li forced himself into a jog, needing to put more distance between himself and Taurin. If only he could do the same to his roiling emotions. Usually, he could control them, as he'd done for decades, yet when it came to Taurin…

A strange aura brushed over him. Li came to a sudden stop, all senses on alert. He looked around saw nothing through the long grass gently swishing in the breeze. His hand went to the handle of his sword. The aura grew stronger, and surprisingly quickly. It was like nothing he'd ever felt before. It wasn't elven nor did it belong to a dwarf. It wasn't like the unicorns' either. He turned to face the direction it seemed to be coming from—still nothing.

A rhythmic sound caught his attention. He looked up, expecting to see a prairie chicken flapping overhead. But what met his eyes turned his blood to ice. Far above him, a dark shape shot through the sky, larger and faster than any bird. Though he'd never seen one in person, there was no mistaking a dragon.

He crouched down in the grass and tamped down his own aura. To his relief the dragon flew by without noticing him. But it was short-lived, for the dragon was headed the way he'd just come.

Taurin.

He took off after it, pushing through the grass, feet pounding against the ground. Taurin had told him they never came this far east, preferring to hunt nuu in the heart of the prairie. So why was one here now?

Only one aura could draw their attention.

Moon.

Li had no idea if dragons ate unicorns, but nothing else could explain it. Yet, how could a dragon sense her aura from so far away? He'd stopped being able to feel it—and Taurin's—not long after he'd lost sight of the stable. Perhaps they had picked up the horn's energy before it had fused with her.

It didn't matter. He had to stop the dragon, to reach Taurin before the magenta beast did.

Calling on his magic, he infused his legs with speed and strength. It was an incredibly draining spell, one not often used, but he had no hope of catching the dragon otherwise.

Li sped across the prairie, eyes on the dark speck ahead of him. To his dismay, it was growing smaller, but that didn't stop him.

It soon disappeared from sight. Li continued, fearing what he would find, his pulse racing as he gasped for air. Despite his heart screaming not to, he ended his spell, not wanting to run out of magic before he reached the yard. He'd need it to fight the dragon; a sword alone wouldn't be enough.

After far too long, the hazy shapes of hills appeared in the distance, the very ones he'd wandered aimlessly in for days after being shipwrecked. Which meant the stable was just ahead. Energy surged through him.

A bone-shattering roar rent the air, and the dragon's aura suddenly grew stronger. Li's stomach twisted with dread. That could only mean one thing: they had stopped.

The smell of smoke filled his nose. He coughed as he ran towards a wispy plume rising in the air, growing thicker and darker by the moment.

Shit.

The endless grass finally opened up. Li was a seasoned warrior; he'd been in many battles and seen his share of blood and gore, he'd seen villages razed and crops reduced to ash.

And yet, none of this prepared him for the destruction before him.

The yard was ablaze, dark smoke billowing high into the sky. The fence around the pasture burned in a few places. Horses galloped past him, nearly knocking him over, their eyes rolling with fear.

He frantically looked around, trying to take in everything at once. "Taurin!"

A loud flapping overhead drew his attention—the dragon. At the sight of the beast, a sort of calm settled over him. This was no different than any other battle. In fact, this one would be easy: there was only one target. One large, flying, fire-breathing target.

Taurin had once told him a dragon's scales protected it from most magic. Those words echoed in his head as he drew his sword. This blade, gifted to his mother decades ago by the imperial family, had been enchanted to amplify magic. It would only withstand a few uses, so Li was determined to make them count.

The surface of the blade rippled as he poured his aura into it before it began to spark and crackle. The best way to deal with a flying target was to remove them from the sky. Arm extended, he swung his sword back behind him, as if to throw it, then snapped it forward without letting go. Lighting exploded off the blade, hitting the beast before it knew what was happening. The strike bounced off their scales, flying off into the distance.

The resulting boom shook the ground, nearly knocking Li off his feet. He held his breath as the dragon hung in the air. Had it not worked? Had its scales still blocked the spell? The massive wings suddenly crumpled.

The dragon hit the ground.

Li didn't waste any time, quickly closing the distance. Blade still crackling, he slashed at its shoulder. His sword glanced harmlessly off the scales, but the dragon screeched as lightning tore through it again.

It whipped its head around, teeth bared. It was hard to tell if his magic was doing damage or simply annoying the beast.

Regardless, he didn't back down.

"Li!"

The familiar voice pierced him.

"Stay back!" he shouted, gaze locked on his opponent. Distraction would be fatal.

Faster than expected, the dragon was on its feet, its head nearly reaching the top of the barn.

Like a serpent, it struck out at him, jaws open wide to reveal dagger-like teeth.

Li hopped to the side and brought his sword down on its neck. The resulting peal of metal against scale made his ears ring. The blade left no mark.

The dragon drew its head back. Li ignored it, leaping out of the way as razor sharp claws slashed at him. He charged his sword with lighting again, and there was a sudden drain on his energy—he was running low on magic. Damn. Not only did his sword's enchantment have a limit, but he had only a few good spells left in him before he had to rely entirely on steel.

The dragon opened its mouth, a spark in its throat the only warning Li got before a torrent of fire shot forth. He sprinted away, counting how long the blaze lasted. Though the dragonfire had missed him, a section of the paddock fence had been set ablaze. The part that suffered a direct hit was quickly reduced to ash, while others snapped and crackled as the fire spread. There was nothing he could do about it now.

A spiked tail whipped towards his head, just as lethal as the rest of the dragon's arsenal. Li had half a thought to stop it with his sword but leapt away instead—a wise decision. The tail struck a wooden wheelbarrow, reducing it to splinters.

The sight of everything he and Taurin had worked hard to build destroyed filled him with rage. And try as he might to tamp it down, lest it cloud his mind, he could only see red.

Letting out a battle cry, Li charged the dragon's side. His sword struck its leathery wing, unleashing another bolt of lighting, and, to his surprise, slicing through the thick membrane. The dragon's pained roar nearly deafened him.

It did have a weakness.

The dragon spun around to face him, the injured wing tucked tight against its side. Red rivulets of blood ran down it. That would stop it from flying.

He darted to the side, hoping to land another blow on its wings, but the dragon wasn't going to let that happen again. Its maw opened wide. Flames spewed out.

Li's chest burned as he ran, barely keeping ahead of the searing heat.

A cry of despair sounded over the rush of fire. From the corner of his eye, he saw something gold dart towards the stable. His heart plunged.

The barn was on fire.

A terrible scream came from inside—Lily and Moon.

Li wanted to rush in after Taurin, but he had a dragon to deal with. At first, he'd only wanted to drive the beast off, but everything had changed.

Letting out a war cry, he charged the massive, scaled monster.

The dragon's magenta scales rippled with gold from the light of the flames, but Li found no beauty in it as he got in close—closer than he should—and slashed his sword across its good wing. He grunted as the blade struck one of the long, thin bones, but was rewarded with a gush of blood and a deafening screech.

The wing suddenly snapped open, flinging him off like an irritating fly. Li rolled across the ground, absorbing most of the impact. Thankfully he'd managed to hang onto his sword.

He hardly made it to his feet before lethal jaws came at him again. Awkwardly leaping back, Li narrowly avoided being bitten in half.

Too late, he realized it was a ruse. A cry left his lips as the dragon's tail smashed into him. He hit the ground, sword flying from his grasp.

Burning pain erupted across his ribs. Had he been impaled? No, that didn't feel right. He must have been cut. Decades of training allowed him to push the hurt aside. More troubling was that he was nearly out of magic and had lost his sword. *Shit.*

Ignoring the blood seeping from his wound, Li rose to his feet—and not a moment too soon. An inferno blasted towards him.

Li leapt out of its path, intense heat washing over him. He scanned the area for his fallen blade as he ran around the dragon to avoid the torrent of fire. Something glinted near its scaled feet.

Of course that's where it had landed.

He had two options: he simply could run in and try to grab it, knowing his wound was slowing him, or he could use the last of his magic to try to distract the beast while he retrieved it. Magic he would need for a killing blow.

The answer was obvious. Steeling himself, Li ran in.

His opponent had no desire to let him pass unchallenged. The dragon came at him with tooth and claw, keeping him away.

I don't have time for this! He needed to help Taurin!

Avoiding another lethal lash from its tail, he realized it avoided touching his sword, which still shone brightly with the light of their fire. Too brightly, given the fact it was in the dragon's shadow.

The dragon was still turning after missing him with its tail. Li shot forward like an arrow, risking a bit of magic to aid his sprint.

Claws swiped at him, but he threw out his arms and dove over them, somersaulting as he hit the ground—right to his sword. He wrapped his hand around the hilt and was immediately buffeted with a fiery aura that threatened to overwhelm him. Li had no chance to contemplate it; the dragon was on top of him.

But he didn't need to.

Still enhanced by his speed, he threw himself out of the way of dagger-like teeth. Before the dragon could lift its head, he slashed the blazing sword across the side of its throat, cutting through scales like butter.

The dragon wrenched its head up with a strange gurgling sound. Crimson blood poured from the wound, splashing on the ground in a hot rain. The beast tossed its head to and fro, body thrashing as it fought against death's cold song. It reared up, mouth open in a silent, defiant cry, before crashing down.

It didn't move again.

Li, covered in sticky blood, was already racing towards the burning barn. Caught up in the fight, he didn't know if Taurin had made it out, but he didn't see his beloved golden elf, nor Lily and her foal anywhere. A loud creaking and groaning drew his gaze up.

No!

His heart stopped as the roof of the barn collapsed.

Chapter Nineteen

Ash

Acrid smoke filled his lungs and stung his eyes. Coughing, Taurin pressed deeper into the burning barn, praying he wasn't already too late.

He had to get to Lily and Moon.

Fire licked up the walls, hungrily consuming everything he and Li had worked to repair. It leapt for the rafters, floating cinders setting the hayloft ablaze.

The crackling and popping drowned out the fight outside. Though it pained him to leave Li alone, there wasn't much he could do against a dragon. The lives of these two were just as important.

He reached Lily's stall. The mare bucked and reared, kicking at the wall, eyes rolling in fear. Moon cowered in a corner.

Heart racing, Taurin tugged at the door latch, but it wouldn't budge. Panic surged through him, stealing away what little breath he had left. The world began to spin as he gulped for air, chest too tight.

Fuck, not now!

He gripped the latch, knuckles white, and breathed in quick and deep. Between the bite of the metal and his breathing, the spinning slowed. He coughed from the smoke he'd just inhaled, eyes watering.

Lily reared up and screamed. The horrible sound shook every fibre of Taurin's being, but it helped him to pull his scattered mind back together. He yanked on the latch again, but it still didn't move. Lily kicked the door in her frantic attempt to escape, which must have damaged it.

He pushed against the door with his shoulder, hoping to realign it. No luck. Letting out a frustrated cry, he threw his weight against it.

"Come on!"

The latch held fast. Taurin burst into tears. No, he couldn't lose them like this! He had to figure something out. He had to save them. But he wasn't good at stuff like this. He needed Li in here; he'd know what to do. The warrior would—

Right, he had magic. Taurin took a step back and raised a hand towards the door. "Stay back," he told the horses, hoping they would listen. A glowing green orb formed in his palm, its light overshadowed by the flames raging around them. With a sharp cry, he launched it at the latch.

The metal exploded.

"Yes!" He threw open the door, the hinges cracking loudly. Lily and Moon bolted past him, seeking freedom.

An ear-splitting pop filled the air, as if a branch was being torn off a massive tree. Taurin threw an arm over himself as fire rained down upon him.

Before everything went dark, he could only hope Lily and Moon had made it out in time.

His head was filled with bees. He tried to bat them away, but he couldn't move. Ugh, why wouldn't they leave him alone while he was trying to sleep? It was so warm and cozy and why was someone shouting? This wasn't the time for shouting. The noise faded. Taurin welcomed the oncoming oblivion.

"—in!"

The screaming ripped him away from the encroaching serenity.

"Look at me!"

The voice was distant, like the shouter was down a deep tunnel. But it was quickly becoming clearer, and louder, and everything was too hot. It burned. Everything burned. Oh gods.

Taurin's eyes opened, but everything was too bright. He shut them again.

"I've got you," said a familiar voice.

He was being carried.

"Stay with me."

Ah, it was Li. But hadn't he left? Maybe that had only been a terrible dream.

Violent coughs suddenly racked his body. Air, he needed air.

"We're almost there."

Almost where?

Cool air hit him. He coughed again, trying to greedily suck in clean air.

"Put him down over here," said a new voice.

He was laid down on something soft. They surrounded him, but no matter how hard he tried, he couldn't make out what they were saying. That comfy darkness beckoned to him again, and he succumbed.

When Taurin woke, he was in his bed. A dwarf sat on a wooden chair nearby.

"Ah, you're awake!" she said.

"Matil?" His voice cracked, and Taurin thought his throat might crack along with it. He sat up, body screaming in protest as he did.

"No speaking, you need water." She hopped up and poured him a mug of water from the jug on his nightstand. "You drink all of that. I'll be right back. Need to let 'em know you're awake." She gently handed him the mug.

Taurin nearly dropped it. The parts of his hands he could see were raw and red. Bandages covered the rest.

"Easy there," she said. "Drink it slowly. You've been through an ordeal. Now, I'll be right back." She disappeared down the stairs.

Taurin slowly sipped the water. The first mouthful stung going down, but eventually, the water relieved his throat. He put the mug on the nightstand and lay back against the pillows, eyes drifting shut. What had happened to him? The last thing he remembered was blasting off that damned latch.

And then...he bolted upright, hissing as pain pulsed through him. The roof! The roof of the barn had caved in on him. And—

Loud voices below, followed by footsteps rushing up the stairs, drew his attention.

"Taurin!"

Li burst into the room.

"Taurin, are you—? How are you?"

He'd never seen the warrior looking so frazzled before. His normally sleek hair was a mess, and his clothes were torn and covered in soot. A length of bandage was haphazardly wrapped around his torso. From the way it was quickly unravelling, Taurin suspected he'd been in the middle of having it applied. Blood oozed onto it, the most concerning part of Li's dishevelled appearance.

"What happened?" Taurin croaked. He coughed again, clearing his throat.

"What do you remember?" asked Li cautiously. He moved to the side of the bed and knelt.

"Most of it. The dragon, the fire. You running off. I'm assuming the roof collapsed on me?" Taurin hadn't looked under the blankets yet. He feared what he would see. Burns and bandages, no doubt. Though, judging how everything ached, he didn't think he'd lost any limbs. His eyes drifted to Li's weeping wound. "Is that from the dragon? Go finish getting that looked at!"

Li looked like he was about to protest but Taurin's glare had him going back down the stairs.

He sighed and reclined on the pillows, eyes drifting shut once more. What met him wasn't sleep, but the scene of the roof coming down on him. It replayed over and over. He gave up and opened his eyes, hoping Li would return soon.

More footsteps came up the stairs, but from the sound, he knew it wasn't Li.

"I've brought you some soup," said Matil. "Do you need help?"

"I can feed myself, thank you." He took the offered bowl.

"Li will be back in a moment. Grimmst is just finishing patching him up. Could have been done sooner if he'd just sat still. Suppose that's my fault for letting him know you were up."

Taurin forced a smile. While he appreciated the chatter, he really just wanted to talk to Li. What had happened to Lily and Moon? Were the rest of the horses alright? Why had he left?

"You eat that up," said Matil, stern but not unkind. "You need your strength to recover."

Taurin began to eat. The stew was nothing special but filled him with a nice warmth—nothing like the fire that had nearly consumed him.

He was nearly finished a second bowlful when Li returned with Nellie tucked under his arm. The bandages around his chest were now wound tightly in place, the only thing covering the upper half of his body. He'd changed into some clean, loose pants. Though his hair was still a mess, at least his face had been washed.

"You're looking better," said Matil, taking Taurin's bowl. "Now, you two behave." She waggled a finger at both of them before heading downstairs.

"What happened to the dragon?" Taurin asked, too afraid to bring up their fight and Li's sudden departure. Was he going to leave again? Taurin couldn't bear the thought.

"I dealt with them," Li replied, moving to sit on the edge of the bed, careful not to brush up against his legs under the covers. He set Nellie down, and she immediately made herself comfortable beside Taurin.

"Did you kill them?" he asked hesitantly, petting Nellie. Her presence, like Li's, was comforting. He was glad she had survived the attack. Killing a dragon usually took a handful of nobles; perhaps one of the royals could do it alone or with a partner.

"Yes," replied Li, "though it was no easy feat."

Taurin imagined not, given the extent of Li's injuries. "How?" Nothing Li had ever done indicated his abilities rivalled that of the royal family.

"With much difficulty and honestly, luck. My mother's sword helped to amplify my magic, bypassing the dragon's natural intolerance. The blade itself worked on their wings, until I was disarmed. At some point, the dragon hit the blade with their fire, and it reacted to what little magic was left, giving the blade the properties of dragonfire. With it I was able to cut through their scales, ending their life."

Silence fell over the room, save for the occasional peep from Nellie. Taurin's mind buzzed. He'd never heard of a sword doing that. "I'm glad you survived."

"So am I. This scratch," Li looked down at the bandages, "is the worst wound I sustained. It's nothing compared to what could have happened."

Taurin shivered, not wanting to think about that. He slid one of his hands closer to Li and felt calm settle over him when Li covered it with his own. "When did the dwarves arrive? Did you call for them?" Taurin wasn't sure when Li would have had time to send them a message.

"No, they saw the dragon flying overhead and followed it. Since there is nothing out here save for us, they suspected something was up."

"And they were right."

Li nodded. "They showed up just as I defeated the dragon. Not only have they been tending to our wounds, but they helped put out the fires."

"Did they haul me out of the barn?"

"No, that was me. The shield you conjured protected you from the worst of it, but I fear had I been a moment later, you wouldn't have made it."

"I'm glad you came back," said Taurin, the beginning of a smile on his lips.

The warrior looked away.

Taurin's smile vanished before it came to fruition, something unpleasant squirming in his gut. "I need to know, what did I do to upset you? To make you—"

"I'm sorry." The warrior pulled his hand away.

Taurin's heart thumped, worried Li would vanish into thin air before his eyes.

"You didn't do anything," Li said, running his hand through his dark hair, messing it up even more. "So you have every right to be angry with me. I would be in your position. I should have told you everything instead of feigning anger and running off."

"Told me what?" He drew his hands into his lap and picked at his nails. Li's words that morning had hurt him just as much as Vardis' betrayal.

Li went quiet for a moment as he gathered his thoughts.

Taurin waited, the nail picking keeping him sane.

"The Cloud Empire is after me," Li started.

Taurin looked up from his hands, heart pounding. "Why?"

"I was on that ship because I was fleeing the empire. Everyone aboard was a deserter."

The word hung in the air. Li, a deserter? Taurin couldn't believe it. He was so brave, so noble. "Why did you leave?"

Li closed his eyes for a moment, gathering his thoughts before he spoke. "We disagreed with the Cloud Empire's ways. They were using us against our own people. If a farmer didn't send in a certain amount of their crops, we would be ordered to fetch what was deemed missing, even if the low yield was beyond their control. Other times, we would be dispatched to settle disputes, ordered by those above us to use unnecessarily drastic and violent means that only further antagonized the people instead of creating a resolution.

"Eventually, a bunch of us had had enough, but we weren't in a position to fight back or make change at a higher level. So we planned our escape, fleeing while patrolling the coast. The storm that hit was no ordinary storm. The empire conjured it in an attempt to wipe us out. And as you know, they nearly succeeded."

Taurin reached out and put a hand on Li's shoulder. The warrior relaxed under the touch. "I think what you did was very brave," he said. "I never would have been able to do something like that." He wished Li had told him sooner but said nothing; it wouldn't help.

"That's not all," Li continued, voice dropping to a near whisper. "My parents died during a border skirmish, but given my mother's prowess in battle, I suspect more was at play. An officer showed up in my camp one day and pulled me aside. She told me they had fallen in the north during a routine patrol. That the northerners had ambushed them." Li's voice cracked.

Taurin wanted nothing more than to wrap a comforting arm around Li's waist but refrained due to the warrior's injury. By the gods, Li had gone through so much.

"The officer held out my mother's sword as proof," Li continued, leaning into Taurin's touch. "I was too shocked at the time to process the details of what she told me. I simply accepted the sword and her reminder never to turn it against our own people, lest I be deemed a traitor. At the time, her warning didn't seem strange, but once the fog of loss and shock lifted, I realized it was out of place. Obviously, turning any blade against your own people makes you a traitor."

Taurin nodded in agreement. "The same goes for here." Usually. While Vardis hadn't intentionally wanted to harm their people and their home, letting Taurin take the fall for their mistake made him a traitor in Taurin's eyes. It was Vardis who had been experimenting with magic. *I was only trying to stop him! He's the one who should be out here, not me.*

But then, he never would have met Li.

"The entire story surrounding their deaths was vague," said Li. "While there had always been tension along the northern border, a tactic like an ambush was out of character for our neighbours. At first, I told myself that they were resorting to new techniques because their strength wasn't as great as ours, but after speaking with some of the other...unhappy warriors, they agreed it was strange. Unfortunately, we had no way of investigating the matter. I asked to be sent up north, under the pretense of wanting to protect the empire from those who had killed my parents, but my request was denied."

Taurin frowned, gently rubbing Li's shoulder. "That's suspicious."

"Yes. It didn't fill any of us with confidence. There was no reason to deny my request—unless they had something to hide."

"But why would the empire kill them?" said Taurin incredulously. "It sounds like she was one of their best warriors!"

"She was," said Li, a steely glint in his eyes. "I think—I think my mother's power scared the imperial family. Her strength rivalled theirs. Given how she treated everyone with understanding and compassion, it would have been easy for her to turn most against them."

"But did she want that?" asked Taurin, eyes wide.

Li shook his head. "Not that I know of. But it does make me wonder..." He sighed. "Not long after the visit from the officer, we decided it would be best to leave soon. We worried the empire would start keeping a closer eye on me and my troop. So, the next time we were stationed near the sea, we acted. And the rest you already know."

"So," said Taurin, removing his hand from Li's shoulder, "you think the empire is still hunting you down."

"I know they are. It's not like them to let their prey get away."

"How? They must think the storm killed you." Taurin crossed his arms.

"They'll check," said Li matter-of-factly.

"How are they going to search the entire ocean?" He raised a brow.

Li opened his mouth, then closed it.

"Exactly. I'd say you're pretty safe over here."

"They might be able to track my aura."

Taurin snorted. "Unless they were right behind you, your aura on the beach would have faded by now—if they'd even been able to track it after the magical storm."

Li didn't look entirely convinced, but his face softened. "Perhaps. I said those hurtful things to you because I didn't want you to follow me. I was worried that if the empire found me here, they would hurt you."

Taurin's heart melted. Li didn't hate him. He'd left out of concern. Out of love.

Taurin leaned forward, ignoring his protesting body, and kissed him on the cheek. "Now that that's settled, tell me what happened to the herd. Are Lily and Moon alright?"

Li turned to face him, and his expression made Taurin uneasy. "The dwarves have been trying to track them all down," he said slowly. "We lost Sparrow. We found her remains in the pasture."

Taurin gripped the blanket, heart aching.

"We've put everyone we've found in the stallions' pastures for now, since they weren't as heavily burned."

"But what about Lily and Moon?" Taurin asked again, throat tightening.

"We haven't found them."

Taurin let out a small sigh of relief. "So they weren't in the barn."

"No, they made it out before it collapsed. But what condition they're in, I cannot say."

"That's...that's okay. They'll come back. They won't want to be away from their herd." He had to believe they would return. He couldn't bear the thought of losing them.

"The dwarves have one of their sorcerers, Hazel, the one who made the magical letter, with them, so I did my best to describe Moon's aura for her to track. Hazel and her partner been out all morning searching." For once, Li didn't sound confident.

"We'll find them," said Taurin, not letting himself believe otherwise. After all they'd done to save the little filly, they couldn't lose her now.

Chapter Twenty

Anew

A day passed before Taurin was well enough to leave the cottage. Li helped him apply cream to his burns, heart twisting at the sight of his red, angry flesh.

Matil stayed with them to help with the horses and oversee the hunt for those who were still missing. All but Lily and Moon had been found.

Li had an arm protectively around Taurin as they gazed upon the destruction the dragon's fire had wrought. The barn's roof was gone, and the walls were charred black. It would have to be torn down and built anew. The paddock fence had been incinerated in a few places, but that would be an easy fix once Taurin was well enough to wield his magic. For now, ropes and planks were filling the gaps, allowing the horses full use of the space. Deep gouges scored the ground between the paddock and the barn, evidence of Li's fight against the dragon.

Taurin's form shook as tears rolled down his face.

"It's alright," said Li. "We can fix this."

"How?" asked Taurin. The hopelessness in his voice pierced Li's heart. "The barn is ruined, and Moon and Lily are missing."

He knew Taurin wanted nothing more than to join the search for them, but he wasn't well enough to ride a horse. "What else is missing from this scene?" He soothingly rubbed Taurin's side.

Taurin was silent for a moment, trying to figure it out. "Where's the dragon?" he eventually asked.

"Well, dragon parts are very valuable, so I offered them to the dwarves in exchange for helping us rebuild. And those you already owed have also claimed some of the remains, so that debt has been repaid. You are now free to sell all three foals."

Taurin looked up at him, eyes wide in disbelief. "You're lying. There's no way—"

Li cut him off with a gentle kiss.

"Oi, you two!" shouted a gruff voice. "Get outta the way so the wagons can get through!"

They broke apart and moved as wagon after wagon rolled by, all carrying building supplies.

"Li, you're..." Taurin's words died as hope lit up his face.

"Everything will be fine."

Within a few hours, the dwarves had torn down the ruined barn, salvaging what they could for other projects, and burning the rest.

Li couldn't believe how efficient they were. By nightfall, the new barn frame was built. It would be larger than the old one, something Taurin had requested. While it wasn't big enough to shelter the entire herd, it now had twelve stalls instead of six.

"Why do you need so many stalls?" asked Li.

"Just in case," was all Taurin said.

Li cocked his head. Once Taurin found buyers for the foals, he'd be returning to Sylandris, wouldn't he? Failure aside, Taurin had no reason to stay here once the foals were gone.

Despite how well the rebuild was going, Taurin was still on edge. Moon and Lily had yet to be found. It took everything Li had to stop Taurin from saddling up a horse and going after them himself. But with his injuries, it wasn't a wise decision.

"I can go look for them," said Li that evening. His wound was better, and he couldn't stand seeing Taurin so distraught all the time.

Even now, Taurin was antsy, pacing around the cottage. He'd been watching the dwarves work and trying to help, but after being yelled at by one of them to rest, Li had taken him back to the cottage to prepare a meal for their helpers. Only Taurin was too fraught with worry to focus on cooking.

Taurin paused. "You'd do that?"

"Of course." Li didn't want to leave Taurin alone, especially not in this state, but maybe it would help him settle down. "We'll finish up here, then I'll go."

Taurin thought about it for a moment. "Your cut has healed enough?" He moved to the stove, suddenly a lot more focused than before.

"Enough to ride Sun. She has the smoothest gait."

"But we haven't ridden her in a while."

"Then all the better, she needs it."

Taurin's brow was furrowed, but he didn't press the subject. Finding the lost pair was too important. "I wish I could come along."

"I do too, but not with your burns. We don't want to aggravate them."

While Li tacked up Sun, Taurin distributed meals to the workers. The outer walls were nearly all up, so about half a dozen dwarves were getting ready to start on the roof.

The build was going smoothly.

Once all the workers were fed, Taurin took the leftovers to Li in the stable. "Here, a snack for the ride," he said, tying a leather pouch to the saddle before giving Li a peck on the cheek. "Be careful. And bring them home."

"I will," said Li, cupping Taurin's cheek gently as they stared into each other's eyes. What a fool he'd been for leaving. If he hadn't, he would have been able to protect everyone from the dragon.

"It's not your fault," said Taurin sternly. They'd had this talk before. Taurin didn't blame him one bit, but Li couldn't shake the dregs of guilt.

"I know," Li sighed, then swung up into the saddle.

Taurin smiled at him, his love and kindness filling him with warmth.

Sun's smooth gait was easy on Li's side, which was good. He couldn't afford to be distracted; it took every ounce of concentration he had to focus on Moon's faint aura. Her trail, though only a few days old, was very stale, so he followed Hazel's—the dwarf who had offered to find Moon—aura until he was able to get a good reading on Moon's.

It led him back and forth across the prairie but did seem to be going south.

Towards the unicorns' forest.

Was Moon seeking out her sire? It was a possibility, though the foal was so small and so young. It was unlikely she had the strength to get that far.

Hazel's aura wove across the land more than Moon's did; she'd clearly had a tougher time following her path, and Li had to concentrate on not getting sucked into following it instead. He'd done so already and lost valuable time.

Li rode on, growing more concerned by how much distance the tiny filly had covered. Sure, she had her mother by her side, but this wasn't normal for a horse. This had to be because she was part unicorn. His only consolation was that both her aura and Hazel's were growing steadily stronger.

He crested a roll in the land.

"Whoa," he said to Sun, bringing her to a sudden stop.

The ground before him was all torn up, with dirt sprayed everywhere and the grass ripped up or flattened.

Sun shifted her weight and snorted nervously.

"Easy there," said Li, patting her neck. He kept a tight rein on his rising worry, not wanting to unsettle her further. He dismounted and examined a long furrow in the dirt. It looked like a giant claw mark, though not quite dragon-sized, and relatively fresh.

A low sound caught his attention. He frowned and led Sun to a dark mass half obscured by grass.

Immediately, the dwarven aura grew stronger.

"Hazel!"

The dwarf lay on her side, eyes closed.

"Hazel?" Li knelt beside her. He kept hold of Sun's reins, not wanting her to wander off.

The dwarf groaned again before opening a bleary eye. "Whozzat?"

"Li, Taurin's partner. Are you alright?" He couldn't see any injuries as he approached, but that didn't mean anything.

Hazel tried to sit up.

Li moved to stop her. "It might be best if you keep still. Let me check you for—"

The dwarf pushed his hands aside. "I'm fine. Just gimme a moment."

Li did, relieved that she was moving well.

Hazel looked around, taking in the destruction. "Ran into a tahter. Darn thing must have smelled dragon on me or somethin'. Started going nuts. Swiped at us and knocked me out of the saddle."

"Wasn't someone else with you?" He stood up and fetched a waterskin from Sun's saddle. The mare kept shifting around uneasily, which was odd given that the tahter was gone. She must not have liked its lingering smell.

Hazel gladly accepted the water. "The aura got muddled at one point, so we split up a while ago," she said before taking a long drink. She passed it back and carefully stood up. "Seems nothing is broken. Anyway, we'd had your filly and her mum when the tahter appeared. Dunno where they ran off to. Mum tried to fight the giant critter off."

Li immediately started feeling around for Moon's aura. He circled the area, trying to determine which way she had fled. But Sun wasn't having any of it. She stomped and snorted, tugging at the reins he held.

"What's going on?" he asked the mare, frowning. This was very unlike her.

"Follow her," said Hazel, coming up beside him.

Li looked between the dwarf and the horse, then nodded.

Sun led them away from the site of the attack. The grass was undisturbed from the fight, but some of the blades were broken, as if something large had come through. His heart leapt. Lily and Moon had come this way, the little filly's aura was growing stronger. She had to be around here somewhere.

Li glanced at Sun. Her nostrils were flared. She could smell her herd-mate nearby.

A grey blob appeared in the grass ahead of them.

Sun whickered.

A head popped up. Lily was standing—a good sign. She approached them, her gait unhurried. A small dark shape followed her like a shadow.

Li nearly melted with relief. They were both alive.

He passed Sun's reins to Hazel and approached the pair.

"Hey girl," he said to Lily, holding out some fruit. The mare perked her ears toward him and walked over. He picked up the lead rope dangling from the halter Hazel had put on her.

Lily ate the offered snack, undisturbed.

"You two went pretty far." He peeked at Moon, who was all but glued to Lily's side. The foal blinked at him. There was no need to halter her; she would follow her mother.

Li quickly checked them both over, not finding any injuries. Using magic, he cleared a small bit of grass, dug a hole, and filled it with water, letting Lily and Sun drink.

"Mind your ears, I'm gunna call my pony," said Hazel. She let out a short, quiet whistle, then a much louder one that carried across the plains. Li sensed magic in it.

They didn't have to wait long before a stout chestnut pony came trotting up to them. After letting the pony drink as well, Li and Hazel mounted their steeds and turned back towards the stable.

As much as Li wanted to hurry back, all the horses were tired, and he wasn't sure how Hazel was faring after her knock on the head. They took breaks whenever Moon started to slow down, though he was still amazed by the little filly's stamina.

He kept a lookout for Hazel's companion, but the dwarf said she'd have someone reach out to them once they were back.

The sun had long set by the time they reached the yard.

"Li!" Taurin came flying out of nowhere, slowing as he got closer so as not spook the horses. "You found them!" he said, tears rolling down his cheeks.

Li dismounted and pulled him into a tight hug. "I said I would."

Taurin cried into his shoulder. He pulled away to thank Hazel for her help, then took Lily's lead.

A dwarf named Orik, whom Li didn't recognize, came up to offer to give Moon and Lily a thorough health check. Li let them go while he untacked Sun.

"You did very well," he told the mare, brushing her down. She flicked an ear at his praise. He turned her out into the pasture before joining Taurin.

"They seem sound," Orik said as Li approached. "Can't see or feel any injuries, and neither seems dehydrated. They just need a rest, 'specially that little one."

"I really appreciate you looking at them," said Taurin.

With a nod, Orik went to join the others at their makeshift camp near the barn.

"We should put them in the field with the others," said Li. "I see you repaired the fence while I was away."

The woven branches had been filled in with new greenery, and the mares were back in the large pasture. They turned Lily and Moon out in the smaller pen the other foals had occupied. It was Moon's first time meeting the herd, and they didn't want any accidents after just getting her back.

"I'd rather put them in the barn, but..." said Taurin.

"They'll be fine. The dwarves will be here if anything happens." Li put an arm around his waist. Taurin leaned into the touch.

"I suppose you're right." He gently kissed Li on the cheek. "Now, let's get you to bed."

Yes, this is definitely home, thought Li.

And if the empire ever came knocking, he would deal with it.

Chapter Twenty-One

Together

Over the next few days, the new barn was completed, a brilliant marvel of craftsmanship that dwarfed the old, cramped structure. Taurin shook his head as Li, despite his protestations, kept trying to help with the repairs.

"My scratch is healed enough!" Li had called out from the roof. Taurin had been tempted to climb up there himself and drag him down.

"It's more than a scratch!" But Taurin smiled despite his concern. He understood Li's drive; he hated to stand by while others worked and he constantly had to remind himself the workers were receiving payment in the form of the dragon remains. In fact, he and Li were the ones actually losing out by trading them away so cheaply. It was a sore spot, but neither of them minded all that much.

The finished barn was a marvel: twice as big, and far more open and airier. The tack room was an actual room as opposed to an overflowing closet, and the barn's location was reimagined to open directly into the pasture. Thanks to Taurin's manipulations of the surrounding plant life, the rear door guided horses effortlessly into their paddock. No more leading horses across the yard.

"Who'd come up with such a poor design in the first place?" grumped the workers anytime it was brought up.

Taurin just shrugged.

Each day brought new signs of hope. The foals thrived under their care, growing stronger with each sunrise. Taurin had sent word to Lyrellis about the dragon attack, hinting at the existence of a half-unicorn foal that had likely lured in the beast with her strange aura. "That'll catch their attention," said Taurin once he'd finished writing, eyes glinting.

"Won't it draw the Elithar's attention?" said Li, referring to the dragon attack.

"Yes, they'll come to investigate, but we'll use that to our advantage. We'll have offers when the nobles catch wind of Moon's lineage—and they will, trust me."

Li furrowed his brow in thought.

True to Taurin's word, the Elithar arrived just a few days later. An elf with a piercing gaze dismounted a magnificent blue roan stallion, flanked by a warrior on either side.

"Welcome, Captain," said Taurin with a courteous nod before leading the captain into the cottage while their companions took care of their mounts. Nellie followed them inside, clucking her displeasure at the intrusion into her home.

"I would like a full report of the attack," they demanded, ignoring the hen, voice measured and cool. Taurin didn't like how their eyes kept flicking to Li in the kitchen. Would they drive him away for being an outsider? Take him prisoner?

Taurin scooped up Nellie, fearing she might peck the captain. He pushed those troubling thoughts aside as he recounted the harrowing details—how a dragon, drawn by Moon's aura, had attacked the herd, and how Li had bravely fought to save them both.

The captain's gaze grew sharper. "Just how was the dragon defeated?" they demanded, skepticism tinting their tone. "It is...unusual for a single elf to take down such a beast on their own, especially an elf without a drop of royal blood."

Taurin was glad Nellie's feathers hid how his hands trembled. "I—um..."

"I used my sword," Li interjected smoothly, emerging from the kitchen and setting down a tray with tea and sliced fruit. "The enchantments cast upon it absorbed the power of the dragon's fire, allowing me to cut a fatal blow."

"May I see it?" It wasn't a request, but an order.

"Of course." Li nodded and went upstairs to fetch it. He returned a moment later and held it out for inspection.

The captain examined the sword in near silence. Taurin couldn't read their expression as they drew the blade, but he could feel their aura pulsing as they thoroughly examined it.

"I see...I cannot allow you to keep this," they declared abruptly.

A flicker of anger flashed across Li's face—so brief that only Taurin noticed. There was no way Li would hand over his blade. It was all he had left of his mother. Of his family.

"And why not?" Li asked evenly. "I've had it for a long time. It belonged to my mother."

"The aura of this sword far exceeds the strength we allow commoners to wield." They probed further, eyes like bits of ice. A sudden burst of magic emanated from the captain, rocking Taurin and Li's senses, like they'd stepped through a powerful ward. Nellie squawked and flapped her wings, causing Taurin to drop her. She darted into the kitchen.

"Where are you from?" the captain asked.

Taurin frowned. Was this some sort of truth ward?

"The Cloud Empire," said Li, crossing his arms over his broad chest. His calm defiance of the captain's cold scrutiny impressed Taurin, though it was clear the magical aura of interrogation would not end soon. Under their unyielding gaze, Li admitted softly, "I defected, I fled across the sea with some fellow warriors in a storm—I am the sole survivor."

The magical tension ebbed.

"I see," said the captain. "So long as no further trouble ensues, you may remain here, but I am confiscating your blade."

Li stepped forward, brow furrowed. "That's my mo—" A look from Taurin made him stop. It wouldn't benefit either of them to start a fight with the Elithar.

With a curt farewell, the captain rose and turned once again to Taurin. "We will return soon to verify your success with the horses. Good day."

Once the door closed, Taurin went over to Li and wrapped his arms around him, noting how he trembled. "I'm sorry you had to give up your mother's sword."

Li sighed, returning the hug. "It's alright. I suppose I don't mind losing it if it means I get to stay with you."

Taurin knew parting with the sword hurt Li more than he let on. But with those words, something Taurin had been mulling over for the last half-moon solidified. Not only was he determined to repay his debt, but he also wanted to purchase the farm, to stay here with Li, until the end of their days. He smiled and pecked Li on the check. "Thank you."

The farm was quiet once the dwarves packed up and left, but it didn't last long. A letter arrived from one of the noble families expressing keen interest in Moon. Word of the half-unicorn had spread like wildfire, and soon, inquiries poured in.

"We'll have to hold an auction," said Li one morning over tea and scones, feeding bits to Nellie under the table. "If that doesn't violate the rules of your punishment."

"No, no," said Taurin, "an auction is allowed. They would be attendees, not visitors. But let's wait to see if the royal family makes an offer first."

Yet after nearly half a moon, no letter bearing the royal seal came. Despite this, Taurin found buyers for Han-Han and Breeze's foals, the offers between forty to fifty gold.

"There's something we need to talk about," Li said the morning of Moon's auction. The two of them, aided by Matil and Tagna, had just finished tidying up the yard. They had Lily and Moon tethered in the barn, giving them both a thorough grooming. "What do you plan on doing once you're finished here?"

Taurin's gaze fell on Moon as he gently brushed a stubborn patch of dirt from her dark coat.

"Originally, I intended to go back home," said Taurin slowly. "But now...now I don't want to leave. There's nothing for me beyond my past. I've come to love this place, these horses—this life." His words trembled with quiet passion. "I'm hoping that whatever we get for Moon not only repays what's owed but lets us keep this farm. For us."

Li's smile softened his features, and with it, a deep certainty bloomed within Taurin. Though the idea of a future together in this beloved place was tentative, it was the first promise of a life built not on debt and duty, but on love and shared dreams.

By midday, the yard had transformed into a vibrant gathering ground. Dozens of nobles—elves and dwarves alike—milled about, sipping drinks and sampling sweets. Long, tiered benches had been magically conjured by Taurin and Li to face a small showing pen erected in front of the barn. Matil took up her position as auctioneer at the table set up beside the pen, joined by one of the Elithar overseeing the event.

As the auction commenced, Taurin took a steadying breath, then led Lily and her foal into the pen. His hands shook as he adjusted the mare's lead rope. Anxiety pricked at him—were Moon's delicate horns too strange? Would they mar her beauty, her potential, in the eyes of these highborn bidders? Yet, when he caught Li's reassuring gaze, his determination returned. He circled Lily slowly around the pen, Moon bouncing gaily along beside them.

The murmurs of noble appraisal grew as bidding commenced. Taurin's heart turned to ice when he spotted a familiar face among the crowd: Vardis. *What's he doing here?* Taurin clenched the lead rope with shaking fists as Vardis persistently outbid every offer. The thought of losing Moon to someone like him made Taurin's stomach turn.

Li, ever vigilant, leaned in close as Taurin circled by. "He won't win," he murmured fiercely, tone brooking no argument. Taurin suspected Li would punch the bastard out if he did.

"Can I see one hundred and twenty gold?" hollered Matil.

Vardis raised his marker; Taurin's heart clench.

Someone immediately outbid him, but that didn't deter him.

As the price rose higher, more disappointed nobles dropped out. Soon only two remained: Vardis, and an elf from the powerfully wealthy Highleaf family.

Vardis raised his marker, countering their latest bid.

The Highleaf raised theirs.

Vardis countered again, offering two hundred and fifty gold.

The other noble hesitated.

"Are there any other bids?" asked Matil, scanning the crowd just in case someone was missed. "Going once."

Taurin's chest tightened up. No, Vardis couldn't win!

"Going twice." Matil's words were a dirge that struck him to the core of his being.

A flash of brilliant gold cut through the charged air.

All the elves stood at once, turning towards the approaching riders. Even from a distance there was no mistaking the insignia on their golden outfits.

The royal family had come, led by none other than Princess Solinian Goldensky. In intricate golden attire, she dismounted with regal grace.

"I do hope I haven't missed the sale."

"N-no Your Highness," Taurin stammered.

The princess and her entourage made their way to the seats, a row of nobles scuttlling out of the way to make room for them right at the front. "My apologies for arriving so late," said the princess. "Please, continue with the bidding."

Matil repeated Vardis' last bid of two fifty. "Any other offers?"

The princess raised a marker, offering a thousand gold. The crowd went dead silent.

"Any other offers?" asked Matil. "Going once."

Taurin held his breath. Vardis couldn't match that, could he?

"Going twice."

He stared at Vardis, sweat rolling down his cheek.

"Sold!" cried Matil.

The crowd clapped, the polite sound distant to Taurin's ears. His heart, however, soared knowing the royal payment would settle his debt and secure the farm's future.

After the auction, Taurin let Princess Solinian into the pen to meet Moon.

"Hello, little one," said the princess, holding her hand out to Moon. The foal sniffed her before pressing close to her mother.

"She's a bit shy," said Taurin, fighting to keep his voice steady. Now that the auction was over, he just wanted to collapse. He didn't even have the energy to be awed by the princess' presence.

"Shy, or perhaps overwhelmed from being put on the spot," said the princess. She gently scratched Moon's neck. "Her horns are fascinating. I heard the rumours, but seeing them in person is different."

"Using the remaining funds," Taurin said awkwardly, "I would like to purchase this place. I want to stay here and raise horses with my partner." His eyes flicked to Li, resolute.

"With your debt repaid, I see no issue with this," Princess Solinian replied. "I will have the paperwork drawn up as soon as I return to Lyrellis."

"Thank you," said Taurin, blinking back tears, fighting to keep his composure in front of royalty.

"My condition is this: should any more foals like Moon be born, please notify the royal family at once. I've heard unicorns mate for life." On that note, she rose. "It is time to return home. Someone will fetch Moon once she has been weaned."

"O-Of course, my lady. I'll inform you straight away!"

The two sat atop of the tiered bench, watching the sun set over the paddock. Now that the crowds had departed, the yard was quiet. The horses grazed peacefully in the field, and the chickens had been returned to their coop. It had been a perfect day—aside from Vardis—but he'd been satisfyingly thwarted in the end.

Li drew Taurin close and looked down at him, pride filling his eyes.

"What?" Taurin asked, blushing under the intensity of Li's expression.

"I'm just so proud of you. You did it," Li whispered, his voice thick with emotion as he nuzzled against Taurin's cheek.

"No," Taurin replied, "we did it—together." His voice trembled as tears blurred his vision. "I couldn't have done any of this without you. I owe you so much."

Li brushed away the tears, smiling warmly. "I wouldn't be alive right now if you hadn't brought me into your home, so I think we're even." Li kissed him then, softly, their breath mingling in the small space between them. But as the gentle kiss rapidly grew to something heated and passionate, Li's hands tangled in Taurin's hair, Taurin's arms wrapping tightly around him.

"Barn or bed?" Li asked between kisses, his voice low and suggestive.

"Bed," Taurin replied breathily as he nipped at Li's lips.

Arms still wrapped around Li, he all but dragged him up the stairs into the candle-lit bedroom. His lips met Li's in a heated kiss once they passed through the door.

Muscled hands roved over the planes of his back. Taurin shivered beneath Li's touch and pulled his hips close in return, Li's need pressing against his own. Stepping forward, he forced Li down onto the bed, mouths still sealed together.

Everything beyond the cottage faded away—no debts, no dragons, no pregnant horses to worry about—as the two entwined in an unspoken promise. Each kiss, each touch was a declaration of the trials they'd overcome and the future they would build together.

They broke apart only to shed their clothes, Taurin all but ripping the garments off both of them. He stared down at the muscled warrior beneath him with hungry eyes, lips parted.

"Like the view?" asked Li, a teasing smile on his lips.

"Who wouldn't?" replied Taurin. Li's figure put all his sketches to shame. It was as if he'd been sculpted by the gods themselves. Taurin ran a hand down Li's broad chest. The way the warrior's breath hitched sent heat straight to his groin. How could he ever hope to capture such perfection?

"Careful, you don't want to cut yourself," said Li, eyes dark with desire.

"On what?"

"My chiselled abs," Li smirked.

Taurin snorted, then dipped his head to nip at Li's neck.

Li groaned, eyes lidded. "Fuck, Taurin."

"Patience," he said playfully, "we're getting there." Taurin awkwardly reached over to the night stand and fished out the bottle of oil, applying a generous amount to his fingers.

"Wait," said Li suddenly.

Taurin paused, his slicked hand reaching for Li's member.

"Usually, you're the one taking," said Li, "but we can switch it up. I enjoy it both ways."

Taurin's heart thudded in his chest. It had been a long time since he'd been the one on top; Vardis had never given him a choice.

"Only if you want to," Li said quickly. "If you're not comfortable—"

"No, I'd like to do it," Taurin quickly replied.

Li smiled. "It's been a while, so try to be gentle..."

"Of course!" The last thing he wanted to do was accidentally hurt Li. He'd never forgive himself if he did. He applied more oil to his hand just to be safe. "Flip over."

Li gave him a curious look before rolling onto his stomach.

Taurin grabbed Li's hips and raised them, spreading his legs to give himself a full view of Li's assets. He swallowed.

"Are you alright back there?" asked Li impatiently, face pressed into the pillow.

"I'm just admiring the goods." He rubbed a slicked finger against Li's entrance. Li immediately stiffened up.

Carefully, Taurin eased it inside. There was a sharp intake of breath. "Been that long, huh?"

"A few suncycles," came Li's strained reply.

Taurin slowly worked him loose, adding fingers when he could. His other hand dipped under Li to rub his hard length.

Li hissed through his teeth. "Shit..."

"Seems I haven't lost my touch," said Taurin, breathy.

What little restraint he had quickly crumbled away with each of Li's small gasps and moans. He removed his hand and oiled up his aching need, pressing himself to Li and rubbing against the mounds of his ass; his efforts were rewarded with a quiet moan from the warrior. He marvelled at how the hard muscles of Li's back flexed and stretched, reacting to *him*.

Gripping Li's defined hips, Taurin slowly pressed in, groaning as tight heat squeezed him. "Fuck, Li."

The divine noise Li made sent a shudder through him. Gods, it had been too long since he'd been in this position.

"Fuck is right, get on with it, Taurin," huffed the warrior.

Taurin wasn't about to deny him. Mimicking the slow press of his hips, he slid one hand down Li's back, tangling it in the long, silky locks cascading over the warrior's strong shoulders, pooling on the sheets like dark ink.

Li, taking him all in, shuddered.

Slowly, Taurin moved his hips, groaning at the sensation. Taurin didn't know what was more arousing: filling the warrior or the sight of him trembling and panting beneath him. Regardless, he wasn't going to last long.

Working up a steady rhythm, he tugged at Li's hair, curious.

Immediately Li tightened up around him, breathing sharply. "Taurin—"

Not told to stop, Taurin did it again, harder, timing it with a snap of his hips.

A loud, deep moan filled the room. "T-touch me," Li stammered, clutching tightly at the sheets.

Taurin's other hand slipped under Li, gripping him gently.

The world ceased to exist as their bodies moved as one, the intensity of their passion deepening in the candlelight. The sounds of their heavy breathing and lovemaking filled the room. Nothing else mattered but the two of them.

"Liander..." Taurin breathed as he repeatedly sheathed himself to the hilt. Another tug of Li's hair caused him to tighten deliciously, nearly pushing Taurin over the edge. "Gods!"

"Taurin, I'm—" Li was cut off by a moan, body going taught as a bowstring as his release crashed over him.

Taurin gave one last, deep thrust before everything went white as a sudden release of pressure swept his mind away.

Panting like he'd just sprinted across the plains, he collapsed on top of Li, face buried in the dark hair that had brought both of them so much pleasure.

Li mumbled something, pulling him from his euphoria-induced daze.

"What?" asked Taurin, voice hoarse.

The warrior shifted, and Taurin slid in beside him.

"I love you," said Li softly, dark eyes like liquid pools.

Taurin pulled Li close, nuzzling his neck. "I love you too." He breathed in Li's musky scent, tasted the sweat on his skin, overjoyed at the thought of spending the rest of his days with the man he loved—the man he'd saved who, in an exquisite turn, had actually saved him.

Acknowledgements

First off, a huge thank you to Laura who read and reread my manuscript so many times. This book would be terrible if not for your invaluable input! Thank you to Bee for beta reading for me again! Shoutout to Leen, Ash, and Laura for giving me constructive feedback on the cover design and illustration. And finally, thank you to my editor, Michaela.

ALSO BY

The Crystal Chronicles – Young Adult Fantasy (ages 13+)
The Hidden Crystals
The Twin Moons

About the Author

R. Dawnraven is a formless entity who enjoys collecting skulls, swinging swords, and creating all kinds of art. They live on treaty 1 territory, and have a BA in East Asian Languages and Cultures. *Reins of Magic* is their third novel.

Tiktok – Bluesky – Instagram – Tumblr

@RDawnraven

Photo by author.

www.ingramcontent.com/pod-product-compliance
Lightning Source LLC
LaVergne TN
LVHW041629060526
838200LV00040B/1509